Kate knew he was going to kiss her, but was she ready for this?

Was it still too soon? There had been no one else for her since the day she had met Liam, and she still wasn't sure, was uncertain how she would react, afraid that she would be unable to respond to another man.

But at the touch of Tom's lips something magical began to take place; whether the result of the moonlight, the wine, or the chemistry between the two of them, she had no idea. But as her lips parted beneath his, and his fingers became entangled in her hair, she found herself not only responding to him, but also becoming acutely aware of the awakening of some long-forgotten desire deep inside.

Dear Reader,

In *A Very Special Surgeon,* I have returned to the
Eleanor James Memorial Hospital—or Ellie's as staff
and patients alike affectionately know it—this time
to the busy routine of the obstetrics and maternity
department.

I wanted to explore the theme of love a second time
around. When a marriage ends, whether in the death of
a beloved partner or in divorce, the aftermath can be
devastating for the one who is left. Often, the idea of
new love can seem a remote possibility, especially when
children, struggling to come to terms with problems of
their own, are involved. Sometimes, however, love can be
right there where it is least expected, just waiting to be
discovered.

For Kate Ryan, widowed at a young age, and for
Tom Fielding, recovering slowly from a bitter divorce,
working alongside one another for years, love, when
it comes, is a delightful surprise.

I very much enjoyed writing about Kate and Tom, their
respective children and their joyous discovery and I
hope you will have as much enjoyment reading about
them.

With very best wishes,

Laura MacDonald

A Very Special Surgeon

Laura MacDonald

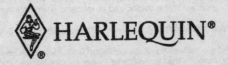

TORONTO • NEW YORK • LONDON
AMSTERDAM • PARIS • SYDNEY • HAMBURG
STOCKHOLM • ATHENS • TOKYO • MILAN • MADRID
PRAGUE • WARSAW • BUDAPEST • AUCKLAND

ISBN 0-373-06462-4

A VERY SPECIAL SURGEON

First North American Publication 2004

Copyright © 2004 by Laura MacDonald

www.eHarlequin.com

Printed in U.S.A.

CHAPTER ONE

'MUM, who's that man? He keeps looking at you.' Siobhan turned from the bowling lane, making way for her brother Connor to have his turn.

'What man?' Kate Ryan, who had been retying the laces of one of her hired bowling shoes, looked up at her daughter.

'He's over there—three lanes down. He has a boy and a girl with him. Oh, he's behind the pillar now.'

'Oh, well done, Connor,' called Kate. 'Another strike. At this rate you're going to beat me and Siobhan hands down.'

'Look!' Siobhan grabbed her arm. 'There he is, and he *is* looking at us.'

Kate turned in the direction her daughter was indicating. There was indeed a man in the lane three away from their own, and he did have two children with him—a girl around Siobhan's age and a boy a little older—but at first glance, in his denims and sweatshirt, it didn't register with her who he was. When he straightened up after scoring a strike of his own and his gaze met hers, she felt a little shock of recognition. 'Oh,' she said, 'it's Tom.'

'You know him?' said Siobhan.

'Yes,' Kate nodded, 'it's Mr Fielding.'

'Tom Fielding?' Connor looked up quickly. 'Isn't he your boss?'

'Well, he's head of my department,' murmured Kate.

'He's coming over,' said Siobhan. 'I said he kept looking at us, didn't I?'

He was indeed coming over and Kate found herself tuck-

5

ing a few stray strands of hair behind her ears, suddenly conscious that she looked a mess—hot and dishevelled after the energetic game of tenpin bowling—a far cry from how she looked at work in her smart navy blue sister's uniform.

'Hello, Kate,' he said—he usually called her Sister—a rare smile lighting up his face. She had always thought of him as a rather serious man, but that was at work when he was caring for expectant mothers and delivering their babies and he was wearing his white coat or theatre greens. This was now, when he was off duty and relaxing. 'I thought that was you,' he added, 'but I couldn't be sure.'

'Hello, Tom.' She smiled back. 'Are you enjoying your game?'

'Very much, although I fear my son, Joe, has beaten us all hollow.'

'Must be something about sons,' replied Kate with a laugh. 'I rather suspect mine has done the same. Have you finished your game?'

'Yes, we have. How about you?'

'Mum and I have one more frame each,' said Siobhan. 'Go on, Mum,' she urged.

With a little grimace Kate selected her ball, wishing fervently that Tom Fielding wasn't standing there watching her. It unnerved her having him there.

'Oh, well done, Mum,' cried Connor. 'It's a good one. No...not quite...' he added as only two pins fell. 'Never mind, better luck with your second ball.'

At last it was over and Kate gave a sigh of relief. As Siobhan bowled her last ball, Tom Fielding's two children came over to join them.

'Go on,' Tom said, turning to them, 'tell me the worst.'

'I won,' said Joe.

'Now tell me something I didn't know,' said Tom with a laugh.

'You came second,' Joe added.

'And I was last,' said the girl, her mouth turning down at the corners.

'Don't worry,' said Kate, trying to make her feel better. 'I'm pretty certain I was last as well.'

'Yes, Mum, you were,' said Connor with a grin, looking up from checking the scores.

'Kate,' said Tom, slipping one arm around the girl's shoulders, 'this is my daughter, Francesca. Francesca, this is Mrs Ryan, she's a sister on the maternity unit at Ellie's.'

'Hello, Mrs Ryan.' The girl looked up at Kate from beneath a mass of dark hair. 'Do you deliver babies as well?'

'Yes, Francesca, I do,' Kate replied.

'And this,' said Tom, 'is my son, Joe.'

'Hello, Joe.' Kate smiled at the boy and was thrown slightly by the boy's rather serious grey eyes that stared back at her, uncannily like his father's. Solemnly he held out his hand and shook hers. Kate turned to her own children. 'These are my children,' she said, 'Siobhan and Connor.' Nods and murmured greetings were followed by a slightly awkward silence, as if no one could quite think of what to say next. It was on the tip of Kate's tongue to ask whether or not Tom and his children came bowling often but mercifully Tom himself saved her from uttering such a banal remark.

'We were just going for a pizza,' he said. 'Would you like to join us?'

'Oh, no. No, thank you…it's all right,' Kate began, suddenly flustered at the thought of such a thing. What would the girls at work say if she told them she'd been eating pizza with the great man himself?

'Please,' he said, 'we really would like you all to join us—wouldn't we, guys?' He turned to his children who gave polite nods. Kate glanced at her own children, fully expecting them to be looking awkward and itching to get away from these people who, after all, they'd never met before. Instead, to her amazement she detected an air of if not exactly eagerness then certainly interest.

'We *could* go, Mum.' It was Siobhan who settled the matter. 'We don't have to get back straight away.'

'What about your homework?' asked Kate weakly.

'Done it,' said Siobhan.

'And Chloe, weren't you going to ring her?' Siobhan had nearly declined the bowling trip in order to chat to her friend Chloe, who was away for the weekend, visiting her grandparents.

'It's all right,' said Siobhan airily, taking her mobile phone from her pocket. 'I'll text her.'

'So, is that settled, then?' Tom raised his eyebrows.

'Well, it seems like it.' Kate smiled. 'Thank you,' she added, suddenly worried that it might have seemed obvious that she hadn't wanted to go. 'It's very kind of you.'

'Not at all,' he replied. 'It's nice for Joe and Francesca to have company. And me, of course,' he added. 'I worry sometimes that they find the whole thing a dreadful bore when they come to me for the weekend.'

Kate had been desperately trying to remember what Tom Fielding's situation was. Now his words had confirmed that, as she had thought, he was divorced and his ex-wife apparently had custody of his two children. 'I'm sure that isn't the case but, yes, I do know what you mean—it isn't easy, being a single parent.'

While they had been talking they had changed from the hired bowling shoes into their own and were heading towards the pizza restaurant at the rear of the vast leisure complex. Siobhan and Francesca seemed to be swapping details about mobile phones while Joe and Connor were so deep in conversation about the intricacies of the game they'd just had, it was as if they'd known each other for years instead of only a few minutes.

After finding a table for the six of them, Tom ordered the pizzas and drinks, and while the children were engrossed with a driving game on a machine in the far corner of the room he slipped into the seat beside Kate. 'It must have been very hard for you,' he said quietly, 'adapting to single parenthood. I haven't found it easy, but for you it must have been a thousand times worse.'

'Well, yes, I suppose so,' she agreed. 'But on the other hand, I sometimes doubt I would have got through it all if it hadn't been for the children. They were my reason for living in those awful dark days—they were the reason that made me get up in the morning when it would have been so much easier to pull the duvet over my head and stay in bed.'

'Your son, Connor—he looks like you,' said Tom after a moment.

'Well, yes, at least everyone says he does, although you can't really see it yourself, can you?' She turned and looked towards her son. Then, her gaze moving to her daughter, she added, 'And Siobhan—well, there's no doubting whose daughter she is. She's the image of Liam with her colouring, and I have to say she has the fiery Irish temper to match—a sudden flare-up, but then it's all over.'

'I only met Liam once,' said Tom taking a mouthful of his drink.

'Oh,' said Kate quickly, 'when was that?'

'It was years ago at some do in the hospital social club. I can't remember what it was exactly—someone leaving, I expect. But I do remember you were there with your husband...'

'No,' said Kate slowly, 'it wasn't a farewell do. I remember now. It was a New Year's Eve party and, yes, you're right, I was there with Liam. And you were there with…with…'

'With my wife,' he finished the sentence for her. 'Yes, you are quite right. A lot of water has flowed under the bridge since then,' he observed. 'My divorce…'

'And Liam's accident,' she finished for him when he hesitated.

'It was terrible what happened,' he said softly, 'I was so sorry, we all were…'

'Yes, I know.' Kate took a sip of her own drink, gulped and set her glass down. 'It was one of those chances in a million. Liam had travelled that same stretch of road on his motorbike every night at the same time for years, but on that particular night the road was wet and there just happened to be an articulated lorry on that notorious bend…'

'He was a fine policeman—I remember reading the reports commending him at the time.'

'Yes, yes, he was.' Kate swallowed. It still hurt to talk about Liam even after all this time.

'How long is it now since—?'

'Two years,' she interrupted.

'Two years?' He raised dark eyebrows and for a moment Kate was afraid that he was about to add, 'As long as that?' People did say that, implying that time flew by, but to Kate the two years since Liam's death had been the longest of her life. But Tom didn't say that. Instead, he remained silent, waiting for her to say something more.

'So…so how long have you been on your own?' At last she found her voice. She knew it had been some considerable time. There had been gossip and speculation at work, of course there had, but the subsequent events in her own life had overridden everything that had happened or indeed was happening around her.

'Nearly five years,' he said.

'And the children don't live with you?' Her gaze wandered to the little group clustered around the game machine—her own two, the dark-haired boy with the serious grey eyes and his younger sister with the pretty name and a face to match.

'No,' he said, 'I'm afraid they don't. I wish they did but it was decided that it would be more practical for them to live with their mother.'

'But you do get to see them often?' There was a touch of anxiety in her voice now, as if she couldn't contemplate being apart from her own children even for the shortest of periods.

'Yes,' he said quickly, almost as if he was trying to allay her fears, 'yes, I do.' He stopped, hesitated, then seemed compelled to add, 'Maybe not as often as I would like but, yes, quite often.'

At that moment the children returned to the table and shortly afterwards their food arrived—huge, deep-pan pizzas with a variety of delicious toppings.

While they were eating Siobhan asked Joe which school he and Francesca attended.

'We go to Waterhouse,' he replied, referring to a well-known private school about ten miles outside Franchester. 'What about you?'

'Oh, I go to Franchester High,' Siobhan replied, 'and Connor is still at junior school—but he'll be coming to the high school in September, won't you, Connor?'

Connor, who had his mouth full of pizza, only managed a mumbled reply, which gave no indication whether or not he was looking forward to going to his new school.

Ice cream followed the pizza, and when at last it was time to go Kate found herself amazed that she had enjoyed herself so much. If anyone had told her beforehand that she would be sharing a meal with Tom Fielding and his children she would never have believed them and, indeed, would hardly have relished the prospect of spending part of her precious off-duty weekend with a senior member of the team she worked with.

'Thank you,' she said as they walked to the car park together. 'It was a lovely meal.'

'Perhaps we'll see you here again,' said Joe, as Kate unlocked her rather elderly car. His remark was addressed to them all but his eyes were on Siobhan as he spoke.

'Yes, maybe.' Tossing back the wild cloud of her auburn curls, Siobhan slid into the rear seat while Connor scrambled into the passenger seat beside Kate.

They watched as the Fielding family walked to their own vehicle—a new red four-wheel-drive—and Tom activated the central locking system with a remote control.

'Wow, look at that,' sighed Connor as the lights flashed. 'I wish we could have a new car—couldn't we, Mum? We've had this one for ages.'

'Yes, I know we have,' Kate replied briskly, 'but it still goes, it still gets us from A to B, so I don't see any need to change it.'

'I know,' Connor began as the Fieldings waved to them as they drove out of the car park, 'but it would be cool to have something like that.'

'We have far more important things to spend our money on than new cars,' Kate replied firmly as she started the engine.

'I bet they live in a huge house as well,' said Siobhan, 'don't they, Mum?'

'Don't they what?' asked Kate as she concentrated on joining the traffic on the dual carriageway. The Fieldings' car was already out of sight.

'Live in a huge house, the Fieldings?' Siobhan repeated impatiently.

'I don't know.' Kate shook her head. 'I don't know where they live.'

'But I thought he was your boss. Surely you must know where he lives,' Siobhan persisted.

'Yes, Tom Fielding is in effect my boss,' Kate replied, 'in that he is the consultant obstetrician on Maternity, but I don't know very much else about him. Today was probably the most we've ever spoken to each other outside work matters. He's a very private man. I knew he was divorced from his wife but I didn't know for sure until today that his children live with their mother.'

'Do they?'

Kate glanced in her rear-view mirror and saw that her daughter's eyes had rounded in surprise. 'That's what he said.' She nodded.

'That's a posh school they go to,' said Connor. 'I've seen the children from there—the girls have to wear funny hats!'

'It wasn't so long ago that boys wore hats to school,' said Kate, 'so think yourself lucky.'

'Boys? Hats?' Connor turned to his mother in astonishment.

'Yes. Well, they were caps really, but boys still had to wear them.'

They travelled on in silence, each busy with their own thoughts as they reflected on the unexpected turn of events their weekend treat had taken. When they were almost home Siobhan spoke again. 'Mum,' she said anxiously, 'do you think we will be able to see them again?'

'I don't know, darling,' Kate replied, then truthfully added, 'although I have to say it doesn't seem very likely.'

'Come on, Sue, push! That's right. I can see baby's head. Now I want you to pant for a while—just like they taught you at antenatal classes. Yes, that's right.' Kate turned to the rather frantic-looking man who sat beside his partner, holding her hand. 'It won't be long now,' she said cheerfully. 'Probably on the next contraction.'

'I didn't know it would be as bad as this,' he muttered.

'*You* think it's bad?' gasped Sue Richards. 'You should try changing places—then you'll find out what bad is!' Her face crumpled and turned red then puce as a new contraction hit her.

'Right, come on, Sue, a really big push now. Go on, yes, that's right.' Kate moved aside so that Melissa Holmes, a pupil midwife, could assist her with the birth. 'You're doing really well, Sue. Now pant again, that's right. Ah, the head's here,' she said as she gently took the baby's head, turning it slightly and supporting it as slowly she delivered the baby's forehead, face and chin. The contraction had subsided now and at Kate's instruction Mike supported his partner's back and shoulders so that she could lean forward and see her baby's head.

'It looks blue,' gasped Sue anxiously.

'That's quite normal,' said Kate reassuringly. Turning to Melissa, she said, 'Check the cord isn't round baby's neck.' As Melissa carried out her instruction Sue was gripped by a further contraction and Kate guided out the baby's upper shoulder. Immediately she administered an injection of an oxytocic drug to Sue to aid the separation of the placenta, then during a further contraction she delivered the lower shoulder and the rest of the baby's body and lifted it onto Sue's abdomen.

Turning to Mike Humphries, Kate said, 'Come on, Dad, tell Sue what you have.'

A somewhat dazed Mike looked down at his baby with a mixture of awe and shock. 'It's...it's a girl. Sue, it's a little girl!' he exclaimed. At that moment the baby let out a long wailing cry.

Melissa clamped the umbilical cord and Kate looked at Mike. 'Would you like to cut the cord?' she asked.

'Me?' He looked astonished.

'Yes, why not?' Kate handed him the appropriate surgical instrument and instructed him what to do. After Melissa had cleared mucus from the baby's mouth and nose, Kate wrapped the baby in a blanket and passed her to Sue who gave a long, shuddering sigh of pleasure before welcoming her baby with a smile and the touch of her fingers on its tiny scrunched-up little face.

'She's beautiful, Sue,' said Kate. 'Look at those eyes—she's watching you. And that hair. So dark, just like her dad.' For some reason, as she said it Kate had a mental picture of Joe Fielding and how like his father he was, with his shock of dark hair and those serious grey eyes.

And as if on cue, the doors of the labour suite opened and suddenly Tom Fielding was there. No jeans and sweatshirt today but a white coat over a dark suit and with a stethoscope draped round his neck, but the rest was the same—the shock of dark hair was less tousled today and there was a serious expression in those distinctive grey eyes as he took in the scene before him.

'Sister Ryan?' he murmured. 'Is all well in here?' As he spoke, his gaze met hers briefly. In the normal course of events that probably wouldn't have happened—he would have asked his question and she would have answered, professionally and efficiently with no need for eye contact. Today, however, was different, and only she and Tom knew why. In his glance she detected knowingness, a slight sense of familiarity, which most certainly had never been there before.

'Yes, Mr Fielding,' she replied. 'Everything is fine. Sue Richards has just delivered a beautiful daughter—do we have a name yet?' She glanced at Sue, whose head was bent over her baby, and at Mike, who was looking shell-shocked and still very pale.

'Alice,' Sue replied, 'Alice Marie.'

'Congratulations.' Tom Fielding nodded and smiled first at Sue then at Mike.

'That's a lovely name.' Kate moved forward again. 'Right, Melissa, we have a placenta to deliver.' When she turned round again, once the afterbirth had been safely dealt with and Sue was feeling more comfortable, and while baby Alice was being weighed and measured, she found that Tom had gone. Momentarily she felt a stab of something, disappointment maybe, but why that should be she had no idea. It wasn't as if she had expected him to say anything about their shared meal, after all. But somehow, she supposed, she had been unconsciously hoping that he might.

Half an hour later Kate left the labour suite and made her way to the nurses' station which was situated in the very centre of the maternity suite, surrounded by antenatal and postnatal bays, the labour suites and Maternity's own theatres. Natalie Aldridge, staff midwife and Kate's friend as well as colleague, was seated behind the large circular desk, a telephone receiver tucked beneath her chin as she made notes on a pile of charts on the desk. She glanced up as Kate approached then a moment later replaced the receiver. 'Sue Richards?' she said.

Kate nodded. 'Yes, a little girl—Alice Marie.'

'That's nice.' Natalie nodded. 'Good traditional names for once. We've had two Kylies, a Courtney and a Sapphire in the last week.'

'I doubt Melissa would agree with you.' Kate pulled a face. 'She's just told me she was disappointed with the name Alice—thought it too old-fashioned. So it just goes to show you can't please all of the people all of the time.'

They both laughed, then, growing serious, Kate said, 'Do

you think there might be any sign of a lull in which we could grab a cup of coffee?'

'Your office?' Natalie hopefully raised her eyebrows.

'I was thinking more staffroom,' Kate replied. 'We wouldn't get more than a minute's peace in my office—is there anything imminent?'

'Mrs Broughton is almost ready to deliver but Emily and Rachel are with her and they don't foresee any problem. It is, after all, her fourth baby. We've had a call from Rick Fowler to say his wife is in trouble again. They've spoken to their GP and he's suggested she come in. Mr Fielding knows about it—he was here a moment ago, asked if you were back from the labour suite.' Natalie paused and looked up. 'Oh, here he is now,' she said.

Kate turned sharply and found Tom Fielding at her elbow. 'Oh,' she said, 'you gave me a start. I didn't hear you.' She paused. 'I understand you were looking for me.'

'Yes,' he replied. 'I've been told that Jane Fowler is on her way in. I have a feeling we may have to perform a Caesarean this time—I can't see her going any longer, especially if her blood pressure is raised again. Would you like to be in on this one?'

'Yes, I would.' Kate nodded. 'I know how desperate they are to have a child, and after three miscarriages they've been close to despair.'

'How many weeks is she?' Tom took the folder Natalie passed across the desk to him and began looking through the notes.

'Thirty-four,' Kate replied.

'Then I think we could well proceed.' He nodded and shut the folder. 'I'll see her as soon as she arrives. Do we know exactly when that will be?' He glanced at Natalie.

'About an hour, we think,' she replied.

'That's fine. I have an antenatal clinic now so by the

time I've finished she should have arrived and her observations will be complete.' He started to move away then
seemed to hesitate and glanced at Kate again. 'Good time
on Saturday,' he said. 'Joe and Francesca enjoyed themselves.'

'Yes, so did Siobhan and Connor.' Kate nodded, only
too aware of Natalie's amazed expression.

'We...' He cleared his throat. 'Maybe we could do it
again some time.'

'Yes,' Kate agreed, 'maybe we could.' He went then,
strolling away in his unhurried manner in the direction of
the outpatients' wing.

'Whatever was all that about?' asked Natalie.

'All what?' asked Kate vaguely, knowing full well what
Natalie meant. It was practically unheard of for Tom
Fielding to mention anything remotely connected with his
family or his private life, so when he did it was bound to
be a cause for speculation.

'Him. Mr Fielding,' said Natalie incredulously. 'What
did he mean? All that about Siobhan and Connor and his
children, at least I presume he was talking about his children—Joe and Francesca? Those are their names, aren't
they?'

'Yes, they are,' Kate agreed.

'Well, go on, tell.'

'Come to the staffroom and I'll tell you there,' said Kate.

Kate had a quick word with staff midwife Mary Payne
as to her intentions and whereabouts then led the way to
the staffroom, where she poured coffee for herself and
Natalie, then sank down onto one of the easy chairs facing
the windows.

'Ah,' she said with a sigh as she eased off her shoes,
'that's better.' The maternity and obstetrics staffroom was
a pleasant, south-facing room which overlooked the lawns

and flowerbeds at the rear of the Eleanor James Memorial Hospital—or Ellie's, as it was affectionately known to staff and patients alike. Some patients were sitting in the grounds, taking advantage of the summer sun, either in wheelchairs or on one of several garden seats donated by the hospital's League of Friends. The flowerbeds around the lawns were packed with rose trees of every colour and variety and their scent was easily discernible through the open windows of the staffroom.

'So go on, then,' said Natalie as she sipped her coffee. 'I'm intrigued.'

'There isn't really very much to tell,' Kate replied with a sigh.

'May I please be the judge of that?' Natalie raised one eyebrow.

'We went bowling—you know, to that new leisure complex.'

'You and the children?'

'Yes.' Kate nodded. 'He was there with his children, that's all.'

'That's it?' Natalie looked disappointed.

'I told you it wasn't much.'

'Well, yes, I know, but I thought by the way he spoke you at least might have talked or gone for a drink together or something.'

'Well, yes, we did actually,' Kate admitted.

'What—you talked?'

'Both really, talked and went for a drink—and a pizza as well,' she added after a moment.

'You had a drink and a pizza with Tom Fielding?' Natalie's eyes were like saucers.

'Yes.' Kate nodded then set her mug down on a small table. 'He came over after we'd finished our game. He said they were going for a pizza and asked if we would like to join them. Honestly, Nat, it was no big deal.'

'Maybe not, but, well, you have to admit it's the only time any of us have got even remotely close to the great man. So go on, tell me, what was he like? Was he the same as he is at work? You know, all serious and sort of remote?'

'Yes, I suppose so.' Kate frowned and wrinkled her nose. 'Well, actually, no, now I come to think about it, he wasn't like that at all.'

'So what was he like?' demanded Natalie.

'Well, for a start he was dressed in jeans and a black sweatshirt.'

'He'd hardly be in his greens, would he? Not for tenpin bowling.' Natalie gave a hoot of laughter.

'What I meant was he looked casual, not formal, and he was sort of relaxed in his manner and in his dress.'

'So you went for this pizza—all of you?' Natalie quite obviously hadn't finished.

'Yes, I said that.' For some reason Kate was beginning to feel just a little bit irritated, which was unusual because Natalie didn't usually irritate her—in fact, quite the opposite. It was Natalie who usually made her laugh by making her see the funny side of any situation.

'So what are his kids like? I don't think we've ever seen them.' Natalie seemed unaware of Kate's mood.

'They are nice children—very well behaved. The boy, Joe, is about fourteen and is the image of his father and the girl, Francesca—she's a pretty little thing.'

'And does she look like her father as well?'

'No, not really.' Kate shook her head. 'I dare say she takes after her mother. I can't quite remember what his wife looks like—I think I only saw her once, at that New Year's Eve do at the social club a few years ago.'

'And then they didn't stay long if I remember rightly.'

Natalie sniffed. 'You know she left him, don't you?' she added after a moment.

'Well, I know they're divorced,' Kate replied.

'I wonder why she left him,' Natalie mused. 'Do you think it might have been because he was all mean and moody?' She gave a delicious little shudder. 'I quite like men like that. It usually means they have a dark, passionate side and are terrific lovers.'

'Like your Barrie, you mean?' said Kate, throwing her friend a sidelong glance.

'Yes, just like my Barrie,' said Natalie, and burst into laughter. Her husband Barrie was the dearest, kindest man but was definitely of the cuddly, what-you-see-is-what-you-get variety. 'I love my Barrie,' she said.

'Yes, I know you do, so let's forget mean and moody, shall we?' Kate paused. 'Anyway, he didn't come across as mean and moody to me on Saturday—there was a lot of laughing and joking. Although, I have to say—' She stopped.

'You have to say what?' Natalie had been about to take another mouthful of coffee but stopped, her mug poised.

Kate took a deep breath. 'He mentioned Liam…and… and he was very serious…and compassionate.'

'Well, I should hope so.' Natalie continued drinking her coffee while Kate sat in silence for a moment, recalling how kind Tom had been towards her when they had talked about Liam. She still got that little hard knot in the pit of her stomach whenever anyone mentioned Liam, or even if she thought about him, especially if the thought came suddenly when she had been engrossed in something else. Like now. She had been sitting here drinking coffee with Natalie and chatting happily, then she had thought of Liam, mentioned him and there was that knot again. Surely by now it should be different? Would the day ever come when she would be able to think of Liam in the simple, loving way they had shared their lives instead of in anguish?

'So do they?'

She jumped and looked at Natalie. 'Do they what?' she said realising that Natalie had asked her a question and she hadn't even heard her.

'See much of their father? Joe and Francesca?'

Kate nodded. 'Oh, I would think so.'

'They live with their mother,' Natalie went on, 'that much I do know. I heard the great man say as much once when he was talking to someone in Theatre.'

'Yes, maybe, but it looked like they had a very good relationship with their father. I would say they see a good deal of him.'

'What happened after your pizza?'

'Nothing really—we had ice cream to finish off, then we went back to our cars.'

'Didn't he say something just now about doing it again some time?' asked Natalie. She spoke casually, without looking at Kate, but her tone of voice was just a little *too* casual.

'Yes, he did,' Kate agreed, then drained her mug, thrust her feet back into her shoes and stood up. 'But he was only being polite, so you needn't go reading anything into it.'

'I don't know what you mean,' protested Natalie, her eyes widening innocently.

'Yes, you do,' said Kate firmly. 'You know exactly what I mean. You're matchmaking again, Natalie Aldridge, and you can forget it.'

'But, Kate—'

'Don't "but, Kate" me. I know you mean well but I've told you before, I'm just not interested, not in Tom Fielding or in anyone else. I had everything I could have ever dreamed of with Liam,' she said, 'and no one could ever take his place.'

With a deep sigh Natalie stood up and followed Kate out of the staffroom.

CHAPTER TWO

'THE baby is all right, isn't it?' Jane Fowler looked up at Kate with anxious blue eyes.

'Yes,' Kate hastened to reassure her, 'the baby is fine. There's a good strong heartbeat but these pains you've been getting could indicate early labour.'

Jane's husband Rick, who was sitting beside her bed, looked up quickly. 'But Jane's only thirty-four weeks.'

'Yes, and if baby is born now, that would mean it might spend some time in the special care baby unit we have here at Ellie's, just until it is strong enough to go home.'

'Last time this happened, two weeks ago, Mr Fielding said he thought I would have to have a Caesarean birth,' said Jane.

'Well, everything settled down again on that occasion,' said Kate as she checked the blood-pressure monitor. 'It may well do so again now. But if a Caesarean is necessary, you don't have anything to worry about. You will be in the hands of one of the finest obstetricians in the country.'

'Oh, I know that,' said Jane quickly. 'It wasn't that I was worrying about. It's just that I had so hoped to be able to have a natural birth.'

'And you may well be able to,' said Kate firmly. 'Mr Fielding will be here shortly to see you and the decision is his. Ah.' She looked up quickly, 'Here he comes now.'

Tom walked into the four-bedded antenatal bay in that calm way of his and stood at the end of Jane Fowler's bed.

'Hello, Jane,' he said, 'we really will have to stop meeting this way otherwise your husband may start getting suspicious.' His remark, solemnly delivered, relieved the tension and while Jane gave a weak laugh and her husband smiled, Tom took the notes from Kate and began reading them.

'I think,' he said after a moment, 'that I'd better have a little look and see what baby is up to.'

While Kate drew the curtains around the bed, Jane lifted her nightdress, revealing the large swollen mound of her abdomen. Gently but firmly Tom examined her, feeling the position of the baby and the height of her womb. It was something that Kate had witnessed many times before but for some reason, which she was unable to explain, today she found herself watching Tom more closely and the way his strong surgeon's hands moved. They were beautifully shaped hands, square with tapering fingers. Somehow the sight disconcerted her and hurriedly she looked away.

'I'm not going to disturb baby more than I have to today,' he said at last, straightening up. He turned to Kate. 'How is the blood pressure, Sister?'

Kate handed him the chart on which she had recorded a higher than normal reading.

'And what about these pains?' He looked down at Jane again after reading the chart.

'They have been about fifteen minutes apart,' Jane replied, 'and at one time they were really quite strong.'

'Well, what I propose,' he said at last, 'is that we let you rest quietly for the remainder of today then tomorrow we'll review the situation—unless, of course, things progress before then.'

As they moved away out of earshot of Jane and Rick, Tom glanced at Kate. 'This may well mean a Caesarean section tomorrow,' he said, 'but, like I say, we'll give it twenty-four hours before we make a final decision.'

'Is there no chance of a normal delivery?' asked Kate.

'Not with her history.' Tom shook his head. 'I'm only waiting now in the hope that things might settle down again and she may go further into the pregnancy. Now, Sister, do you have anyone else for me to see before I go?'

Kate shook her head. 'No, Mr Fielding,' she replied, 'I don't think so. If I were you I'd get away before anything else happens.'

'Thanks, Kate,' he said. He spoke quietly so that only she heard his use of her first name, something which, in the past and on the ward, he'd never done. But things had changed since then because now, instead of simply a professional history between them, they also had a social history, slight as that had been.

At the end of her shift Kate drove out of the car park past the huge macrocarpa trees on the lawns at the front of the hospital, then down the avenue of magnificent beech trees to the main road. Home for Kate and the children was at Copse End, a tall Edwardian house situated in a quiet lane on the far side of Franchester. The house belonged to Kate's Great-Aunt Bessie, who was elderly, a widow and childless. After Liam's death, when Kate had been wondering how she was going to manage both child-care and mortgage repayments, it had been Aunt Bessie who had come to her rescue. 'Sell your house,' she'd said, 'and come and live here with me. You could have the top two floors and I would live downstairs—it would be my garden flat. I'd like that, the stairs were getting too much for me anyway. The house will be yours one day as it is—so you might as well enjoy it now. The children would have the garden and plenty of space to bring their friends home. And I will always be here when they come home from school.'

And it had worked. Kate was able to keep an eye on Aunt Bessie, fetch her prescriptions and collect her shopping along with her own, and the children had been only too pleased to find Aunt Bessie there in a warm kitchen with a delicious smell of home baking when they arrived home from school when their mother was working a late shift.

It had been a wrench to leave the house that she and Liam had bought. It was a modern house in a quiet cul-de-sac in a new complex, and they had furnished it lovingly. At the time of his accident Liam had been in the process of landscaping the garden and installing a section of decking where they would have been able to enjoy barbeques on a summer's evening. It almost broke her heart even now whenever she thought about it.

Gradually, though, they had settled at Aunt Bessie's. Kate had already loved the house from her many visits there as a child, as did her own children, so the prospect of moving there and making it their home had seemed something of an adventure. From the sale of her own house and the life insurance money she'd received, Kate had set about making the large rooms of the top two floors of the house into a comfortable family home for herself and the children. And somehow, almost without her being aware of it, the move to Copse End and their subsequent life there was beginning to help her to get over Liam's death.

In fact, the more she thought about it, the more she realised just how far she had come since those dreadful dark days following the accident. The shock—the heart-wrenching shock and disbelief that she'd felt when two colleagues of Liam's had come to her to break the devastating news—had been replaced first by anger, awesome anger when she had railed at everything and everyone, including God, for having allowed this to happen, and then the grief, grief like she'd never known. Whole nights spent holding some garment of Liam's while she'd sobbed for hours—quietly so as not to wake the children—soaking her pillow and leaving her facing the next day feeling wretched and exhausted.

And there had been the children's grief to cope with on top of her own. She'd been strong for them at the time, at least she hoped she had, throughout the funeral, the wake that had followed—obligatory for an Irishman—and the memorial service in the cathedral attended by so many of Liam's colleagues. But afterwards she had felt inadequate in dealing with their pain and bewilderment.

And then, when everything had calmed down and life, at least for other people, had got back to normal, she had been left with the seemingly impossible task of rebuilding their lives. They had coped on a day-to-day basis—at least on the surface—but underneath there had been those practical difficulties to overcome.

'We don't need a childminder, Mum,' Siobhan protested when Kate fretted over them coming home to an empty house or when she dreaded a half-term holiday.

'I'll have to do more hours,' she said when the bills carried on arriving with alarming regularity.

And then Aunt Bessie stepped in, and Kate knew in her heart that she would be grateful to her for the rest of her life.

Now, as she drew into the drive of Copse End and parked the car, she looked up at the mellow old brickwork of the house, the wisteria over the front entrance and the laburnum tree casting its shadow on the front lawn, and realised that almost without her having been aware of it, this house really had become home.

With a little sigh she climbed out of the car, shut the door and automatically made her way round to the rear of the house and the entrance to the garden flat, as Aunt Bessie still insisted on calling it. The gardens here were of the true cottage-garden variety, with a mass of flowers growing higgledy-piggledy from the crazy-paving pathway to the distant dark reaches of the bottom of the garden, which ended with the copse that gave the property its name. Tall hollyhocks lorded it over clumps of lupins, and huge white daisies jostled for position with sweet william and night-scented stocks. A large tabby cat lay on the kitchen window-sill, sunning itself, and as Kate approached it opened one eye, stood up, yawned and stretched.

'Hello, Timmy.' Kate began stroking the cat, then, as he rubbed himself against her hand and headbutted her, she laughed before moving on through the open kitchen door.

Aunt Bessie was seated at the kitchen table, chopping vegetables. A radio on the dresser quietly played her favourite classical music, while Connor sat at the far end of the table, his homework books open before him and his mouth full, no doubt with one of the delicious-looking cherry buns that were cooling on a wire tray.

'Hello, dear.' Aunt Bessie smiled at Kate over her glasses. 'Good day?'

'Yes, not so bad.' Kate smiled then paused and listened as through the ceiling came the steady thump, thump of pop music. 'Has that been going on for long?' she asked.

'I don't know,' said Aunt Bessie, 'I hardly notice it.'

'It's been ever since she came home,' mumbled Connor.

'Don't talk with your mouth full, dear,' said Aunt Bessie mildly. Looking at Kate again, she said, 'I've done enough vegetables for your evening meal.'

'You shouldn't,' said Kate. 'You spoil me you know.'

'It's no trouble,' Aunt Bessie replied. 'Besides, it gives me something to do. Cup of tea, dear?'

'Maybe later,' Kate replied. 'I'll just go upstairs and shower and change first.'

As she climbed the stairs the music grew progressively

louder. She found Siobhan lying full length on her bedroom floor, her homework books scattered around her and the deafening music blaring out of her personal stereo system, which was beside her on the floor.

'Siobhan!' yelled Kate, but there was no response. Swiftly crossing the floor, she bent down and clicked the stereo's 'off' button. The sudden silence was a shock, following as it did the assault on the eardrums.

'Hey!' Siobhan looked over her shoulder. 'What did you do that for?'

'It was far too loud,' said Kate firmly.

'But I was enjoying it,' Siobhan protested.

'You are meant to be doing your homework.'

'I am.' Siobhan looked at her books, one of which was propped open before her.

'You can't possibly concentrate with all that noise,' said Kate.

'Yes, I can.' A rebellious look came across her face, a look Kate knew only too well. 'It helps, actually,' Siobhan added defiantly.

'Well, I'll thank you to keep the volume down in future. Besides, it just isn't fair on Aunt Bessie.'

'She likes it.' Siobhan's chin tilted as she sat up and hugged her knees.

'She doesn't have a lot of choice,' said Kate. 'I could hear the music as soon as I entered the house—right down there in Aunt Bessie's kitchen. It's just not on, Siobhan. If you don't keep the sound down I'll be forced to confiscate your stereo.'

'You can't do that.' Siobhan looked aghast. 'That was Dad's last present to me.'

Kate stared at her daughter and felt her heart twist as, at the mention of her father, tears sprang to the girl's eyes. 'I know,' she said more kindly, 'and I won't have to if you just remember to be a little more considerate in future. You aren't the only one living in this house, you know.'

'All right.' Siobhan shrugged then dashed a hand across her eyes. Kate knew that anything remotely concerning her father still affected her daughter badly.

'Did you see him?' asked Siobhan suddenly as Kate turned to leave the room.

'See who?' Kate paused, one hand on the doorknob, and looked down at her daughter who was still sitting on the floor.

'Him. Mr Fielding.'

'Yes, of course I saw him,' Kate replied. 'I work with him.'

'Did he say anything?'

'What do you mean, did he say anything?' Kate had a vague idea what her daughter was driving at but somehow, and for some reason which was unclear even to herself, she didn't want to acknowledge the fact that she knew.

'About us meeting them at tenpin,' Siobhan persisted.

'Well, he may have mentioned it in passing, but that's all,' Kate replied.

'Did he say anything about us seeing them again?' Siobhan obviously hadn't finished.

'Siobhan, you mustn't read anything into what was said on Saturday,' Kate began.

'Why not?' Siobhan demanded. 'If that's what was said…'

'But sometimes people say things they don't mean to be taken literally. They say things like, ''We must do this again some time,'' or, ''Call in if you're passing,'' but often it's just a form of politeness and they don't actually mean it.'

'Well, I don't call that being polite—saying one thing and meaning another,' muttered Siobhan then, when it appeared Kate had no more to say on the subject, she narrowed her eyes and said, 'So was that it, at work? Was that all he did, just mentioned it in passing, the fact that we'd met them?'

'Well...' Kate hesitated. 'He did actually say what Joe said on Saturday about us doing it again some time...'

'There you are, then!' exclaimed Siobhan, and there was a note of triumph in her voice. 'Maybe he wouldn't have meant it if it had been said just once—but *twice*! He must have meant it the second time.'

'Siobhan.' Kate's voice was gentle now, knowing just how easily her volatile daughter could get carried away. 'You really mustn't read anything into this.'

'You're just being mean,' declared Siobhan.

'No, darling,' said Kate gently. 'I'm not, really I'm not. I just don't want you building up your hopes only for nothing to happen, then for you to get hurt.'

'I've had an idea!' said Siobhan, her eyes shining again, but for another reason this time and not with tears.

'Oh, yes?' said Kate warily. She knew all about Siobhan's ideas. 'And what's that?'

'Why don't we invite them over here? We could, you know,' she rattled on excitedly, not waiting for Kate's answer. 'We could ask them for a meal or something—we could even go bowling again first, then they could come back here for supper or lunch or whatever. After all, it is our turn because Mr Fielding treated us to the pizzas.' She paused. 'There!' she exclaimed dramatically. 'Don't you think that's a really cool idea?'

'*I* do,' said a voice from outside the open door. Kate turned and found Connor standing there. She had no idea how long he had been there.

'There you are, then,' said Siobhan. 'Even *he* thinks it's a good idea, so what do you say, Mum? Mum?' she demanded again. When still Kate didn't answer, she said, 'You *don't* think it's a good idea, do you? Honestly, it's just not fair. You don't want us to have any fun. You never do. I wish Dad was here. He let us have fun.'

'I'm sorry, Siobhan,' said Kate wearily. This was the last thing she wanted now after a demanding day on Maternity: a run-in with her daughter over what she did or didn't allow them to do, and how much better it had all been when their father had been alive. 'I do my best.'

'I know.' Briefly Siobhan looked subdued, as if deep in her heart she knew that Kate did as much as she could. 'But couldn't you just ask them?' she pleaded.

'Look.' Kate took a deep breath. 'I'm sorry, but I really can't do that.'

'But why not?' cried Siobhan.

'Yes, why not?' echoed Connor.

'It just wouldn't be right.' Kate shook her head. 'Mr Fielding is head of my department—it simply wouldn't be right for me to invite him and his family here. When we met them the other day I'm sure he was simply being polite when he asked us to join them. I really doubt that it will be something that is repeated. If it is, fine, but it has to come from them. I'm sorry.' She looked from one to the other of her children. 'But that's the way it is and I don't want to discuss it any more. Is that clear?'

'S'ppose so.' Siobhan scowled, and with a sigh Kate went out of the room and into her own bedroom, shutting the door firmly behind her. For a moment she leaned against the door with her eyes closed. She hated it when either of her children was confrontational. It rarely happened with Connor, who was a placid-natured child, but Siobhan had not only her father's colouring but also his volatile temperament. Liam had learnt to curb and control his temper, especially during his years in the police force, but Siobhan was often given to outbursts, which for herself were quickly over but which left those around her drained and exhausted.

On the face of it, maybe it seemed perfectly reasonable to Siobhan that Kate should return the favour and invite the Fielding family to Copse End for a meal, but Kate knew that would be out of the question. She could just imagine the reactions amongst the staff on Maternity if it should get out—and it would be bound to, sooner or later—that she had invited Tom Fielding and his family to her home. It would be seen as presumptuous at the very least, and she shuddered to imagine what the fallout would be. There would be teasing from her friends, especially Natalie, and suspicion from others who would view it as a ploy on her part, using her children as a smokescreen when her real intentions would be to attract Tom's attention to herself.

Tom, she was well aware, was a very attractive man approaching the prime of his life. He was at the peak of his profession and was reaping the rewards. He was also, since his divorce, highly eligible. There had been much gossip and speculation about him on the maternity unit, with more than a few female members of staff trying to attract his attention. The fact that Kate herself was now single would only add to that speculation if she were to pursue Siobhan's idea. And nothing, she thought in a sudden wave of desperation, could be further from the truth. She wanted no such speculation about herself. She doubted she was through with grieving for Liam and even if she were, she would hardly risk her professional standing by trying to attract the attentions of her boss. She had seen it happen before with depressing regularity among members of her staff and the outcome had more often than not resulted in heartbreak. There was no way she wanted to take

that road or even to have others think that might be her
intention.

With another sigh she crossed the room and began un-
buttoning her blouse. As she did so she caught a glimpse
of herself in the pine-framed, oval mirror in the corner of
the bedroom. She stopped for a moment, turned to face the
mirror and critically surveyed herself. She'd lost weight
since Liam's death, she knew that—there were hollows beneath her neck bones that hadn't been there before, and
under her cheekbones—but she hadn't been able to help it.
She'd had no appetite, and it had only been very recently
that it had slowly started to return. Ruefully she found herself wondering if Liam would recognise her now. Even her
hair was different—still dark and glossy but cut shorter,
into a jaw-length bob instead of long, the way he had so
loved it. The only part of her that still looked the same
were the clear hazel eyes, which stared solemnly back at
her from the mirror. With an almost angry little gesture she
turned away and carried on undressing.

'Mr Fielding is going to perform a Caesarean section this
morning so will you, please, prepare Jane Fowler for
Theatre?' Briskly Kate instructed two of her nurses then
went on to ring Paediatrics to request the attendance of a
paediatrician at the birth. She was told that Matt Forrester,
the paediatric registrar, was available and would be down
shortly to scrub up.

'Are you going to attend this one?' asked Natalie, over-
hearing Kate on the phone.

'Yes.' Kate nodded. 'I promised Jane I would.'

'I have to say, she seems quite calm and resigned now
that the time has actually come and a decision has been
made.'

'All she wants now is to be able to hold her baby,' Kate

agreed. Looking at the notes and charts on the nurses' station desk, she asked, 'Are you going to be able to manage out here? There seems to be quite a lot happening this morning.'

'I think we'll be OK,' Natalie replied. 'We have one mum on her way in, membranes have ruptured and contractions are five minutes apart. Emily and Melissa can take that one. Sita Vanerjee is already in strong labour so I shall attend there with Rachel, and Mary is standing by for Adele Rossington.'

'Heavens! Hasn't she delivered yet?' Kate looked alarmed. 'Is everything all right?'

'Yes.' Natalie nodded. 'Contractions subsided. I got Omar Nahum to take a look at her and he said the baby was fine. ''Just taking a sabbatical'' were his precise words, I believe.'

Kate laughed. 'We're so lucky to have Omar,' she said, 'and the mums adore him.'

'And when they haven't got Omar to drool over they have the delectable Mr Fielding—it's no wonder they keep getting pregnant and coming back for more.'

Kate didn't answer, found she couldn't because there was something, just some inflection of tone, when Natalie mentioned Tom that made her wary. It was almost as if Natalie was expecting her to comment or, even worse, that she was including her in the general female reaction to Tom. And Kate didn't want that, it was the last thing she wanted and it had only come about since that absurd sharing of pizza and ice cream. She was beginning to wish it had never happened—it was causing too much trouble. First from her children, who couldn't wait for the performance to be repeated, and now from Natalie, who seemed to be insinuating goodness knows what, and who should know better, knowing as she did how Kate had felt about Liam and how she certainly wasn't ready—if she ever would be—to feel that way again.

Maybe it was her, she told herself briskly as she took herself off to Maternity's theatre in order to scrub up for Jane Fowler's Caesarean. Maybe she was simply reading something into a situation that simply wasn't there. And maybe it was because that thought was uppermost in her mind that she found herself being a little more brisk and efficient that morning, especially where Tom was concerned.

In her theatre greens, clogs and mask, she was scrubbed and ready in Theatre by the time Tom and Matt Forrester arrived, also attired in greens and masks.

'Good morning, Matt.' She smiled at Matt Forrester. 'How's that gorgeous son of yours?'

'Harry is brilliant.' Kate knew Matt was grinning behind his mask. 'There was never another child like him.'

'You wait a few years,' said Tom darkly. 'Wait until he has you out on the rugby pitch early on a winter's morning.'

'Does Joe do that to you?' Kate spoke without thinking then, seeing Tom's surprised glance, wished she'd stayed silent.

'It's been known,' he said dryly. 'Ah, here comes our patient,' he added, saving Kate from further embarrassment.

Jane arrived on a trolley, having received her epidural in the anaesthetic room. Her husband Rick, who was also attired in greens, a cap and a mask, accompanied her. Both looked apprehensive and fearful as to what was about to happen. Kate stepped forward to reassure them, and while Jane was transferred to the operating table she led Rick to a seat alongside his wife, where he could observe if he wished and comfort Jane throughout the operation.

'You both know Mr Fielding,' said Kate. Turning to

Matt, she said, 'And this is Dr Forrester, who is a paediatric registrar. He is here to examine and monitor the baby as soon as it's born.'

'Hello,' said Matt. 'Do you know the sex of the baby yet?'

It was Rick who answered. 'No, we decided we didn't want to know,' he replied.

'So we're all in for a surprise, then,' said Tom as the theatre staff erected a screen across the top half of Jane's body and made the necessary preparations with cross-matching of blood and a link-up to a heart monitor.

'You do know we shall be taking the baby down to the special care unit, don't you?' said Matt. 'It should be a fairly good weight at thirty-four weeks, but just to be on the safe side we like to make sure.'

'Will I be able to go down and see the baby fairly soon?' asked Jane anxiously as Kate began preparing her abdomen for the incision.

'Yes, as soon as you've had your stitches we'll take you down,' said Kate, 'and if you wish, Rick can go straight away with the baby.'

This seemed to satisfy Jane and she fell silent as Tom prepared to begin the operation. Rick had elected not to watch as the incision was made but as Kate moved forward to apply the diathermy instrument to control the bleeding and Tom began to deliver the baby, drawing it out of the uterus in a rush of water and blood, he couldn't resist a look.

'Jane, Richard,' said Tom, 'you have a son. Congratulations.' As Kate clamped the umbilical cord Tom cut it, then Matt stepped forward and took the baby from Tom. He moved to the far side of the theatre where a nurse was waiting to assist him.

'Are you all right, love?' Rick Fowler leaned over his wife and kissed her forehead.

'Yes, I think so,' whispered Jane. 'But the baby…?'

'It's a little boy, Jane. We have a son!' There was a note of incredulity in his voice.

'I know, but why is he so quiet? Why hasn't he cried?' asked Jane.

'He's with Dr Forrester,' said Kate. 'They will be clearing his airways to help him breathe.'

As she spoke Tom removed the placenta and a nurse took it away to examine it to make sure it was intact and that no part of it had broken away.

Jane still looked very anxious and it was only when a sudden wail from the baby broke the silence in the theatre that she relaxed and smiled. After Matt had finished his examination, he picked up the baby, wrapped him in a white blanket and carried him gently in both hands across to his parents.

'Here he is,' he said, 'all present and correct. Just hold him for a moment, Jane, then he must go into an incubator.'

With a look of absolute joy on her face Jane lifted her arms for her baby and very gently Matt placed him on her chest.

'He is all right, isn't he?' asked Rick anxiously as he took one tiny hand in his and watched in awe as the baby's fingers curled instinctively around his thumb.

'He's fine.' Matt nodded. 'But he may need a bit of help with his breathing, so we'll put him in an incubator and take him down to Sister Forrester and her team. Are you coming with us, Rick?'

'Yes, all right.' Rick nodded. Glancing back at his wife, he said, 'I'll be back soon.'

'It's all right,' she said. 'One of us must go with our son. I can't at the moment so it has to be you.'

'Did he say *Sister* Forrester?' asked Jane, as Matt and a nurse, together with the baby in an incubator and accompanied by Rick, left the theatre to go the short distance to the special care baby unit.

'Yes,' Tom replied. 'Sister Forrester is in charge of the special care baby unit, and she also happens to be Matt Forrester's wife. Now, tell me, do we have a name for the baby yet?'

'Yes,' murmured Jane, 'it's Jordan—Jordan Thomas.'

'Ah, good names,' said Tom with a smile as he prepared to close the incision in Jane's uterus and abdomen. 'Don't you agree, Sister Ryan?' His eyes met Kate's over their masks.

'Of course,' she answered, then at something in the expression in those grey eyes she found herself looking quickly away. Once, not so long ago, it wouldn't have bothered her, probably wouldn't even have happened. Now it did, and she wasn't even sure why.

CHAPTER THREE

KATE ate, paused and wiped the sweat out of her eyes. It was hot, too hot for gardening, but she had set herself the task of clearing the weeds from two of the large overgrown borders at the back of the house. Siobhan had been helping her to start with, albeit half-heartedly, but after only half an hour she had suddenly remembered something urgent that had to be done immediately. That had been nearly an hour ago and Kate hadn't seen her since. Aunt Bessie had kept her well supplied with tumblers full of chilled, home-made lemonade but Kate knew her strength was flagging and that the heat would soon get the better of her. Maybe if she really put her back into it she could at least finish one of the borders, she thought, realising now that the idea of two had been far too ambitious. Bending over again, she began digging out the root of a particularly stubborn thistle. Aunt Bessie had wanted to get a man in to do the garden but when Kate had seen what the charges were just for the smallest amount of work she had told her to forget it. Now, as the sun beat down on her shoulders and her back began to ache, she wondered if that wouldn't have been the best option after all.

'*Mum!*'

She jumped, looked up sharply and caught her arm on the sharp prickles of the thistle. 'Damn!' she muttered under her breath.

'*Mum!*' The shout was even more urgent this time.

'Yes?' she called, at the same time sucking at the scratch on her arm, which was bleeding. 'What is it?'

'Phone!' Siobhan's head appeared from behind the hollyhocks. She looked flushed and excited. 'It's for you!' she added breathlessly.

'Well, couldn't you take a message?' Kate said irritably. 'Tell them I'll ring them back.'

'No, Mum, you don't understand. It's him!'

'Who?' Kate frowned wondering who on earth it could be to reduce her daughter to such a state.

'Him!' said Siobhan again. 'Mr Fielding!'

'Mr Fielding!' Kate blinked then stared at her daughter. 'What does he want?'

'I don't know. He wants to speak to you! Hurry up— they might want to meet us again.'

'Don't be silly, Siobhan.' Kate straightened up and peeled off her gardening gloves. 'It's far more likely that he's ringing from the hospital and it's something to do with work.'

'Does he usually do that?' demanded Siobhan.

'Well, no, I've never known him to, but—'

'There you are then! Come on! Hurry!' Siobhan turned and darted back into the house.

'There's always a first time,' Kate concluded feebly, not that she believed it, not for a moment. Tom Fielding would never phone her at home—or any other member of staff, come to that—about work-related matters. She followed Siobhan into the house and up the stairs, answering Aunt Bessie's raised eyebrows and questioning look with a shrug and a shake of her head. Her living room, with its stripped pine floors and deep coral walls, felt cool after the heat in the garden, while the tapestry cushions on the sofa offered a welcome refuge for her aching muscles, but there was to be no respite for Kate. Siobhan was hopping up and down with excitement and even a mildly curious Connor had left

his games console—unheard of on a Saturday morning—
to see what all the fuss was about.

'Go on, Mum.' Siobhan urged her to pick up the telephone receiver from where it lay on the sideboard.

Taking a deep breath, Kate did so. 'Hello?' she said.

'Hello, Kate?' There was no mistaking Tom's voice and
she felt a little tingle deep inside, almost as if she had
doubted that it really had been him on the phone. 'Kate,
it's Tom. Tom Fielding. Look, I'm sorry to bother you, and
on a Saturday morning as well. This is obviously a bad
time—you were busy.'

'I was gardening,' she heard herself say, 'but it's OK—
I was a bit out of breath, that's all.'

'Out of breath?' He sounded surprised. 'It must have
been pretty strenuous gardening.'

'No, not really, only weeding actually, but I had to come
upstairs to answer the phone. I must be out of condition.'

'You live in a flat?'

'Not really—well, sort of...'

'Look, I'm sorry for dragging you away.'

'It was probably the excuse I was looking for to stop,'
she said. 'Anyway, Tom, how can I help you?'

'I was just wondering, well, we were wondering—Joe
and Francesca that is—if you and Siobhan and Connor
would like to come over. It's so hot, and we have the pool
where everyone can cool off. I will also be barbequing a
few steaks later on and I thought, well, I just wondered if
you'd care to join us.'

Her first instinct was to say no, not to let this thing,
whatever it was that had started the previous weekend go
any further. 'That's very kind of you,' she said slowly, at
the same time watching Siobhan and seeing her face light
up with undisguised pleasure. 'I'm sure the children will

be delighted,' she heard herself continue weakly. 'What time would you like us to come?'

'As soon as you like,' he replied. She thought he sounded pleased that they were coming but she couldn't be sure. 'I don't think the weather is likely to change,' he went on, 'but you never know and it would be a shame to waste all this sunshine.'

'All right,' said Kate, 'but you'll have to tell me where you live.'

'Yes, of course. Sorry, I was thinking you knew. It's in a village called Lower Melbury—do you know it? It's about ten miles west of Franchester.'

'Yes, I know where you mean.' Kate took the pen Siobhan handed her and wrote the name of the village on the pad beside the phone. 'There's a church there beside the green…and a duck pond.'

'Yes, that's right,' Tom replied. 'You take the turning to the left of the church and my house is the second on the right. It's called Kingfishers—you can't miss it.'

'Right, well, thank you,' she said. 'We'll be over in, what? Let's see, about an hour or so?'

'Fine, we'll look forward to it. Oh, and, Kate?'

'Yes?'

'Don't forget your swimming gear.'

'What?' demanded Siobhan as Kate replaced the receiver.

'He's invited us over.'

'Yes!' Siobhan punched the air with her fist. 'I knew it! I told you so, didn't I?'

'Yes, Siobhan, you did,' said Kate helplessly. She still wasn't convinced she'd done the right thing in accepting the invitation, but at the same time she wasn't sure she could have coped with the fallout from her daughter if she'd refused. And really, when she thought about it, there wasn't any earthly reason why she should have refused. It was simply a kind follow-up gesture to the couple of hours they had shared and enjoyed the previous weekend.

'Are the others there? Joe and Francesca?' asked Connor, a trifle anxiously, Kate thought, and she found herself wondering whether his enthusiasm was as strong as his sister's. This family, after all, were complete strangers, or rather they had been until the bowling trip, and they quite obviously lived very different lives from their own, with their private schooling and expensive possessions.

'Yes, the children are there,' she replied. 'Mr Fielding said you might like to swim in his pool—'

'They have a pool?' Siobhan's eyes widened.

'Apparently so, and he's going to be barbequing later as well.'

'Oh, brilliant!'

'You'll like that, Connor, won't you?' said Kate doubtfully. 'Swimming?'

'Yes.' He nodded. 'I like swimming.' He had won badges at his school for freestyle and backstroke.

'Well,' said Kate, 'we'd better get ready.' She wasn't sure how she felt about going, couldn't imagine what Natalie and the rest of them at work would make of it— she and her children socialising with the likes of Tom Fielding and his family.

'I don't see why you shouldn't go,' said Aunt Bessie stoutly when Kate went downstairs to tell her what was happening and voiced her misgivings. 'You're every bit as good as they are, and don't you forget it.'

'Oh, I know, I know,' said Kate with a laugh. 'You don't understand, it isn't that—it's just that somehow we're poles apart, if you know what I mean.'

'Only in terms of wealth and position,' said Aunt Bessie.

'Underneath all that, they have the same hopes and fears as anyone else.'

'I just hope the others at work see it that way,' said Kate.

'You don't think they will?' Aunt Bessie frowned.

'There will be those who will think I'm getting above myself,' said Kate bluntly. 'And there will be others who will read something into it.'

'And does that matter?' asked Aunt Bessie.

'Yes,' Kate replied solemnly, 'because I don't want that. I want the children to have fun and that really is the only reason I'm going. I certainly don't want anyone thinking there is anything else in it.'

'Well, dear.' Aunt Bessie smiled. 'I think you should try and enjoy the day yourself. It's about time you had some fun in your life again.'

'We'll see,' said Kate. 'What will you do today? Will you be all right?'

'Yes, of course I will,' Aunt Bessie replied firmly. 'I have some letters to answer then I shall walk down to the post box to post them and I may even call in on Dorothy for a cup of tea.'

'There's the church,' said Connor.

'And there are the ducks on the pond,' added Siobhan.

The village scene was idyllic, as had been the drive through the Sussex country lanes and the other pretty villages they had passed. Here in Lower Melbury white posts linked with black chains surrounded the village green, while beneath an oak tree in the centre of the green ducks and geese preened themselves or slumbered in the cool shade of the branches, protected from the fierce midday sun. A row of thatched cottages stood beside the square-towered church, their gardens a profusion of colour, from hanging baskets overflowing with petunias and lobelia to huge tubs of scarlet and pink geraniums and multicoloured Busy Lizzie.

'Here's the lane,' said Kate, slowing the car to walking pace as she negotiated the sharp bend to the left of the church, 'and the house apparently is the second one on the right-hand side.'

'Here's the first one,' said Connor. 'The Old Rectory— it looks like the next one is some way up the lane.'

They travelled on in silence for some distance then Siobhan gave an excited yelp. 'There it is!' she said. 'Look, you can see the roof.'

A high beech hedge surrounded the house and at the entrance a white-painted, five-bar gate was standing open. The name Kingfishers was inscribed in gold lettering on a black plaque on the top bar.

'I'd say they were expecting us,' declared Siobhan. 'Go on, Mum, drive in.'

'I'm not sure that I should,' said Kate. The sense of unease that had hung over her ever since Tom Fielding's phone call was stronger than ever, but even as she dithered Tom himself appeared in the drive.

'Hi, there!' He raised one hand in greeting and walked to the car. 'You can drive right in,' he said, bending his head in order to speak to Kate through the open window. 'Park alongside the red car.' He looked cool in spite of the heat in shorts and T-shirt, while his hair looked wet, as if he'd just come from the shower or maybe taken a dip in the pool.

Kate nodded and drove through the gates and onto the drive, which swept round to the left. She finally came to a halt beside the red four-wheel-drive, as Tom had instructed her. She switched off the engine and sat for a moment with her arms resting on the steering-wheel. On the other side of the red car was the Mercedes convertible Tom usually drove to work.

'Come on, Mum.' Siobhan had already scrambled from the car.

More slowly Connor followed her. 'Wow,' he said softly, gazing at the Mercedes, 'look at that!'

Kate pushed her sunglasses onto the top of her head and, climbing from the car, stood for a moment and looked at the house. It was a large, double-storey building, its walls whitewashed and its roof tiled in terracotta tiles. Red-leafed ivy climbed up one wall and trailed across the front entrance, while on either side of the black front door a pair of stone lions stood sentinel.

By this time Tom had walked back up the drive and joined them. 'Welcome to Kingfishers,' he said simply. 'Come inside and, please, make yourselves at home.' As he spoke he took the bag containing their swimwear, which Kate had taken from the boot of her car, and carried it to the house, pushing open the front door then standing back for Kate and the children to precede him.

They entered a wide, almost square hallway, its floor tiled in black and coral tiles, its walls half panelled with wood, half painted a soft colour that was not quite white, though neither was it cream. 'Come through,' he said, leading the way through the hall into a sitting room furnished with dark antique furniture and two huge crimson sofas. French doors led into a large sunroom with comfortable-looking cane furniture which in turn opened onto a terrace. 'Joe and Francesca are in the pool,' he added.

Kate was aware of bright sunlight, of a fan that whirred overhead, of blue and coral mosaic tiles on the floor and then, as she stepped onto the terrace, of the bright sparking blue of the pool, of white wrought-iron tables and chairs, of the high beech hedge which enclosed the pool on two sides and of Joe and Francesca as they waved to them from the water.

Francesca immediately swam to the steps and climbed out of the pool, her dark hair and her pink bikini streaming with water as she grabbed a towel and padded across to greet them. 'Hi!' she said. 'We're so pleased you could come. Come with me, Siobhan, and I'll show you where you can change. You go with Joe, Connor,' she said over her shoulder as Joe also climbed out of the pool.

As the children sorted themselves out, Tom turned to Kate. 'Are you desperate for a swim?' he asked. 'Or would you prefer something to drink first?'

'A drink would be nice,' she said. 'This weather makes me thirsty.'

'What would you like? I was thinking of making some Pimms.'

'That would be lovely.' She smiled. Maybe, she thought, a drink would help to relax her. She was still feeling if not exactly uneasy then rather nervous, as if somehow she shouldn't be here in Tom's house. Which was ridiculous really because it wasn't as if she'd invited herself. He had, after all, asked them here. She wasn't, however, under any illusions that he was doing this for her—this was plainly and simply for the children. No doubt Francesca or possibly Joe had been as insistent over a follow-up meeting as Siobhan had been, and Kate herself knew only too well how wearing that could be.

'Make yourself comfortable,' he said. 'I won't be long.' He disappeared back into the house and Kate stepped back into the sunroom where she sat down gingerly in one of the cane armchairs, then felt herself sink into the soft cushions. Maybe, she thought as she looked around her, this wasn't going to be so bad after all. It certainly beat trying to clear the flower borders of weeds. A few moments later the children reappeared, Francesca and Joe still wet from the pool in towelling robes, Siobhan in the turquoise swimsuit which was a perfect foil for her hair and Connor in his dark green trunks.

Within seconds they were all in the water, splashing and shouting with laughter, and as Connor began to streak up and down the pool and the others watched in admiration, Kate felt herself relax a little more.

'That's a fine crawl stroke your son has there.'

Kate looked up quickly and found that, unbeknown to her, Tom had come back into the sun lounge. He was standing beside her, a tray and glasses in his hands, as he, too, watched Connor.

'Yes,' she agreed with quiet pride. 'Connor loves his swimming. Liam taught them both to swim when they were little more than toddlers,' she added.

He took the glasses of Pimms from the tray and set them down on the table then sat down himself in another of the cane chairs. Lifting his glass, he said, 'A toast, I think?'

'Yes?' She lifted her own glass and waited, wondering what he would say.

'To new friendships,' he said.

Surprised, she allowed her gaze to meet his. Then she echoed his sentiment. 'Yes,' she said, and surprisingly found she meant it. 'To new friendships.'

She took a sip—it was delicious—and then set her glass down again. What had he meant by new friendships? Had he meant just the children? Or had he meant themselves? Because, if he had, wasn't that a little strange? After all, they already knew each other, they'd known each other for years, worked together for a long time. But that was as colleagues. This, what he was talking about now, was friendship and maybe the two were very different. On the other hand, perhaps he meant family friendship—

all of them, both families as friends. Yes, that was what he must mean, she told herself as she picked up her glass again and took a second sip.

'Tell me about this gardening that I've dragged you away from,' he said.

Kate stared at him. She'd become so lost in her thoughts that she'd hardly heard what he'd said. 'Gardening?' she said stupidly.

'Yes.' He smiled and settled back in his chair. 'When I phoned you said you were gardening.'

'Oh, yes,' she said quickly, 'I was. I was trying to clear a couple of borders that have become hopelessly overgrown with weeds.'

'They soon get the upper hand,' he agreed. 'Do you have a large garden?'

'Yes.' She nodded. 'Well, it's not all mine actually—most of it belongs to my aunt. We live in part of her house,' she added when she saw his questioning look.

'Hence you being out of breath after climbing the stairs to answer the phone?' He raised his eyebrows.

'Yes, quite.' Kate smiled. 'We have the top two floors of the house—it's a large house,' she added. 'My aunt has the ground floor, or the garden flat as she likes to call it.' She was silent for a moment, the only sound in the sun lounge that of the overhead fan and, from outside, the cries of the children in the pool. When Tom also remained silent, she said at last, 'My aunt invited us to move there after Liam died.'

'And has it worked out?' he asked.

'Oh, yes,' Kate said, 'for all of us really. For my aunt because she was finding the house too much for her, and for us because I was finding life a bit of a financial struggle. And what with trying to arrange child care...' She trailed off, afraid she was boring him with such mundane details.

'It must have been a nightmare for you,' he said quietly.

'I suppose it was at the time,' she agreed. 'Being a single parent is no joke, whatever the circumstances. But, then, you would also know all about that.'

'My situation is a little different,' he said, and Kate found herself thinking it was very different. Not for Tim the juggling of finances or the anxiety of arranging child care.

'My main problem was that I missed them so much,' he said simply.

Kate stared at him. This wasn't at all what she had expected to hear and quite suddenly her heart went out to him. Maybe Aunt Bessie had been right when she'd said wealth and position really didn't count for very much at all. 'Could you not have won custody?' she asked uncertainly. She didn't know the details of his divorce, only what hospital gossip had said, and that was that his wife had left him.

'Maybe.' He shrugged and Kate wondered if she'd gone too far in raising the subject. 'But if I'd done that their mother would have missed them,' he said after a moment.

'Well, yes…but…'

'And they would have missed her,' he added, not giving her a chance to finish. 'I didn't want them to be pawns or weapons in any divorce proceedings and I knew if I fought for custody it could have all become very distressing for everyone concerned, not least the children.'

'That sounds very generous of you,' said Kate slowly.

'Not entirely.' A ghost of a smile touched his mouth. 'On a practical level it was easier for them to live with their mother. The nature of my work means I would have had to employ some sort of live-in carer for the children—at the time we parted Joe was only nine and Francesca seven, so the most logical solution seemed to be for them to live with their mother. I also happen to believe that young children should be with their mothers anyway.'

'Their mother didn't have to work?' asked Kate.

'No.' He took another mouthful of his drink, and as he leaned forward to set the glass down again Kate noticed a small pulse that throbbed at the corner of his jaw, almost as if it stressed him to talk about the break-up of his marriage. 'She didn't have to work. She was able to be at home with the children whenever they needed her.'

'She's fortunate,' said Kate. 'I don't know what I would have done without Aunt Bessie. I had real battles with Siobhan about having someone to look after her. She was adamant she didn't want anyone, but both she and Connor were too young to be left on their own. For a time after Liam died I used to drop them off at Aunt Bessie's on my way to work, or they would go there after school when I was on a late shift. I must say, life has been much easier since we moved there. It means there is always someone in the house when they get home from school, or even if they've just been out somewhere.'

'You weren't worried about letting your own home go?'

'Not really—you see, under the terms of Aunt Bessie's will I'm her main beneficiary so I was able to give up the struggle to find the mortgage repayments without too many qualms.'

'I'm glad that side of things, at least, has worked out for you,' he said.

They were silent for a moment, Kate wondering whether in her nervousness she had divulged too much about herself or simply chattered about things which could have had no interest whatsoever to her host. 'Did you move after your divorce?' she asked in sudden desperation that she hadn't appeared interested in him, then immediately wondered if in talking of his divorce she had overstepped the mark. 'Or

was this...' helplessly she glanced around her as she spoke
'...your family home?'

'No,' he replied, 'we didn't live here.'

Suddenly she was glad—she didn't know why, but she
was—glad that this lovely house hadn't been the scene of
the break-up of his marriage.

'I bought this house a couple of years ago,' he volun-
teered. 'A friend told me it had come onto the market, I
came to look at it and that was that—I knew instantly I
wanted to live here.'

'It's a beautiful house,' she said, looking back as she
spoke into the spacious sitting room.

'Really, it's too big for me,' he admitted, 'but I wanted
somewhere that the children could come to and think of as
their second home.' Draining his glass, he looked across at
Kate. 'Are you ready for a swim yet?' he said.

'Yes, that sounds a lovely idea.' Kate stood up.

'Come with me and I'll show you where you can
change.'

She followed him as he led the way from the sun lounge
into a room with a shower cubicle and a dressing area with
a pink marbled washbasin and a vanity unit.

'There are plenty of towels,' he said indicating a pile of
brightly coloured beach towels. 'I'll see you outside when
you've changed.'

After he'd gone Kate changed from the long cotton dress
she was wearing into a red one-piece swimsuit and a match-
ing cotton sarong, which she tied around her waist.
Suddenly she felt self-conscious about walking out to the
pool area with Tom and his children watching her. It had
been a long time since a man had looked at her in a swimsuit. But that was silly, she told herself. Tom wouldn't be
looking at her, at least not in that way. His only interest in
asking them to his home lay in providing company for his

children. Taking a deep breath, she walked out of the shower room and back into the sun lounge. Through the glass she could see that Tom had joined the children in the pool. They were all playing with a large coloured ball amidst much splashing, shouting and shrieks of laughter.

Connor spotted her first as she stood in the open doorway of the sun lounge. 'Come on, Mum,' he called. 'It's brilliant in here.'

With that Tom also turned. He didn't speak, just looked at her, and for a moment as Kate walked towards the pool, untying her sarong as she went and letting it drop to the ground, she saw an expression in his eyes that she had never seen there before. It was an expression she'd seen many times in Liam's eyes—one of admiration, appreciation maybe. But with Liam it had always been tempered with love and that certainly couldn't be the case with Tom. But there was definitely admiration there, she hadn't imagined that. It gave her the confidence she needed, the confidence she had found lacking. Holding her head high, she turned gracefully and climbed down the steps into the pool, shuddering slightly as the water crept up her body. Turning, with a few long, slow strokes she swam to the centre of the pool to join the others.

In no time at all she was drawn into the game and for the next half-hour the 'girls' fought the 'boys' for possession of the ball and the scoring of goals at either end of the pool. The fun became fast and furious and it did Kate good to hear her children enjoying themselves so much. And when at one point she caught Tom's eye she had the distinct impression he was feeling the same about his own children.

When at last the allotted time was up it was Joe who proclaimed triumph for the 'boys' team. 'We won!' he cried. 'We won!'

'Only just,' Siobhan declared.

'We'll beat you next time,' cried Francesca.

'We'll have to watch out next time, then,' said Tom with a laugh. He looked happy and relaxed in the water with his dark hair wet and spiky, so much so that Kate had to remind herself that this was the same serious-faced man who strode the corridors of Maternity in his white coat or presided so efficiently in Theatre in greens and mask. And here he was, in effect, agreeing to a repeat performance. How she would ever explain any of this to Natalie without her jumping to conclusions, Kate had no idea.

While the children scrambled out of the pool and grabbed towels, Kate took advantage of the almost empty expanse of water and completed a few lengths before flipping over onto her back and floating lazily, lifting her face to the sun.

'It isn't only your son who is a strong swimmer.' Kate opened her eyes and found Tom looking down at her.

'I've always loved swimming and it was something we always did—as a family,' she added.

'You mean your own childhood family or with Liam and your children?'

'Both, really.' It seemed strange, hearing Liam's name on Tom's lips, but not awkward, quite natural, in fact. Treading water, she ran her hands over her hair, slicking it back behind her ears.

'I'm going to get dressed,' he said, 'and start barbequing some food, but you stay—enjoy the water, make the most of the pool while it's empty.'

It was her turn to watch him as he climbed out of the pool. He was tall and well built with powerful thigh and shoulder muscles. His skin was lightly tanned and the light covering of hair on his chest, arms and legs was dark. Liam had been very different. His body hair had been reddish gold and he had been stockier than Tom. But why was she comparing them? She frowned. She'd never done that before, so why now? Maybe it was because she hadn't seen anyone without their clothes recently—and certainly not another man.

Yes, that was it, she thought, the reason for this comparison—what else could it be? She struck out and completed another two lengths of the pool before climbing out and enfolding herself in one of the thick coloured towels.

By the time she'd dressed and made her way back to the terrace, Tom, now in jeans and T-shirt, had begun barbequing while the two girls were carrying salads, bread and cans of fizzy drinks to two of the wrought-iron tables, which had been pushed together to form one large eating area.

'Hi, there!' Tom waved a pair of cooking tongs at her. 'Did you find everything you needed?'

'Oh, yes, thanks. Can I help?' She looked at the girls. 'Where's Connor?' she asked.

'He's playing a computer game with Joe,' Siobhan replied, raising her eyes.

'It's OK,' said Francesca lightly. 'They will be clearing up afterwards—they don't know it yet, but that's the way it works in this house.'

'That's exactly how it should be,' Kate agreed, 'so, like I said, what can I do?'

'I haven't cut up all the salad yet,' said Francesca. 'There are tomatoes and peppers on the side in the kitchen.'

'I'll find them.' Kate made her way back into the house and through to a spacious, lavishly equipped kitchen where she found and prepared the remainder of the salads.

Lunch was as relaxed an affair as the rest of the day, with them all sitting around the large table on the terrace and enjoying the steaks, chicken, sausages and burgers that

Tom had cooked. When it was over, the boys dutifully cleared away and stacked the dishwasher before disappearing once more to their computer games. The girls had long since taken themselves off to Francesca's bedroom, no doubt to discuss clothes, pop music and boys, and anything else that young girls discussed.

Finally Kate and Tom found themselves alone together in the sun lounge enjoying the last of the afternoon sunshine.

'I must say, you have everything very well organised,' she observed, 'especially where the children are concerned.'

'They have their tasks,' he said, 'and usually things run smoothly, as they did today. But I have to say, sometimes they have their moments and the fur flies.'

'I would be concerned if it didn't,' said Kate with a laugh. 'Mine certainly scrap from time to time but I guess that's all part of growing up.'

'To be honest, I'm rather apprehensive about the forthcoming teenage years,' Tom admitted, 'especially when you consider the number of teenage pregnancies we come across in the course of our work. I worry about Francesca, and I'm only too glad that Jennifer is around to guide her.'

'I worry about Connor not having a man around,' Kate confided slowly after a moment. 'He misses Liam desperately and I find myself feeling terribly inadequate...'

'I think you've coped admirably,' Tom said quietly, 'and the future is, well, a case of one day at a time, don't you think?'

'Yes, I guess so.' She gave a little sigh, then, glancing around, said, 'I suppose really we should think about going...'

'Do you have to rush away?' he asked quietly.

'Well, no, not really.'

'Then stay.' His gaze met hers.

'I don't want to outstay our welcome…'

'You won't,' he replied. 'The children are happy for the time being and, besides, I want to talk to you.'

'You do?'

'Yes,' he said. 'I want to tell you about Jennifer.'

'You don't have to,' she said quickly. Kate wasn't at all sure she wanted to hear about his ex-wife.

'Actually,' he said, 'I think I do.'

CHAPTER FOUR

'YOU know she left me.' It was more of a statement than a question but Kate felt compelled to answer.

'Yes,' she agreed quietly, 'I did hear that somewhere.' There was no point in lying or evading the issue. Tom was as aware of staff gossip as she was.

'I've never really spoken of this to anyone,' he said, looking slightly embarrassed, 'but if you will let me, I'd like to tell you.'

It was very quiet in the sun lounge. She could hear a small aircraft outside as it performed aerobatics high above the Sussex countryside. Kate wasn't at all certain why Tom felt the need to tell her about his marriage and its break-up, or why it should be her he should have chosen to tell when by his own admission it was not something he had previously discussed. She only knew as she sat there and listened that it was something he had to do, as if in doing so he was in some way setting the record straight.

'We met at a hospital in Kent,' he said. 'I was a junior houseman at the time and Jennifer was a medical secretary. It was what I believe is commonly known as a whirlwind affair and we were married shortly after I took my finals. I have come to realise, slowly and painfully, that we should never have married.' He spoke carefully and precisely as if weighing and considering each word.

'But surely you were happy at the time?' Kate frowned.

'I was, or rather I thought I was,' he replied, 'but I wasn't aware of the real facts.'

'I don't understand.'

'Jennifer married me on the rebound from a previous relationship,' he said. 'Maybe she thought she loved me—I don't really know. Maybe she even thought she could make it work, but the fact was she was still in love with someone else.' He paused as if struggling to find the right words. 'His name was Max Oliver,' he continued at last, and as he spoke, once again Kate saw that nerve working at the edge of his jaw. 'He was a solicitor in Jennifer's father's law firm—he's since become a very successful barrister. Anyway, he and Jennifer had known each other since their schooldays. I was aware of the relationship but not the extent of it. And I thought that once we'd had children Jennifer would settle down.'

'And did she?' asked Kate.

'I thought she had to start with, and later we heard that Max Oliver had also married. Life went along fairly smoothly for us, although I often doubted Jennifer's love for me. But then we heard that Max Oliver's marriage had broken up. It was the beginning of the end for us and eventually Jennifer left me to be with him.'

'And are they happy?' asked Kate.

'I think so. Who knows?' He shrugged. 'The children sometimes hint that it is a stormy relationship—but it was what she wanted.'

'But what about you?' Kate frowned. 'What about your feelings in all this?'

'Well, I loved Jennifer at first,' he said slowly, 'of course I did, otherwise I wouldn't have married her. And I really wanted our marriage to work. I guess I'm a bit old-fashioned there, because although we weren't married in church I happen to believe that marriage is for life...'

'I don't think that's old-fashioned at all,' said Kate. 'I believe it, too.'

'The only thing is, that for it to work, I also believe there has to be love, and unfortunately it wasn't me whom Jennifer loved.' He spoke calmly, without a trace of self-pity.

'How did you feel when she left?' asked Kate curiously.

'Hurt, angry, betrayed, bitter, I suppose.' He shrugged. 'But you get over these things in time—learn to live with them if you like.' He paused, his gaze meeting hers. 'You have to, otherwise you'd go insane.'

'Yes,' she said slowly, 'I suppose so.' She was not at all sure how she would have coped with such betrayal—heaven knows, she'd been through pain losing Liam, but at least she had always been secure in the knowledge that he had loved her.

Tom was silent for a moment and then, his eyes finding hers, he spoke again. 'My problem now is that since my divorce I've found it incredibly difficult, maybe almost impossible, to trust anyone again.'

'I would say that's completely understandable in the circumstances,' she replied. 'I would feel the same way in your shoes. I was just thinking, I don't know what I would have done if Liam had betrayed me—I think I would have gone to pieces...'

'No, you wouldn't,' he said levelly, 'because you also have children and, like me, you would have kept going, if only for their sakes.'

'Maybe.' She shrugged. 'But I would still have found it very difficult. Why, as it is...' She trailed off, uncertain how to continue.

'As what is?' he asked quietly.

'Oh, nothing, it doesn't matter.'

'No, please, tell me—this, after all—' a smile played around his mouth '—seems to be turning into confession time.'

She laughed. 'All I was going to say was that I've found

it bad enough since Liam died.' She hesitated, wondering how much she should tell him, how much she should bare her soul. 'One of the managers in Administration at work asked me out about a year afterwards,' she went on at last. 'I was dubious. I didn't want to go, but the girls on the unit persuaded me, said it would do me good, that I needed to get out, all the usual…'

'And did you go?'

'Oh, yes, I went.'

'And?'

'It was an absolute disaster. He quite obviously had only one thing on his mind and I couldn't…I simply couldn't…not after Liam. I had loved Liam so much, we'd had years together…and there was this…this comparative stranger expecting me to…to…' She broke off, unable to continue.

'I understand,' he said simply.

'You do?' She stared at him.

'Oh, yes,' he replied gently, 'more than you think.'

Shortly after that, the children returned to the sun lounge and Kate told them it was time they went.

Tom, Francesca and Joe came out to the car to say goodbye, and as she drove away Kate glanced in her rear-view mirror and saw that Tom was standing in the drive, watching them. Briefly she wondered what he was thinking. Was he pleased to have his home to himself once more or had he enjoyed the day as much as she had? Was he regretting having told her so much about himself and his failed marriage, or was he relieved to have unburdened himself?

'We'll have to do it now,' said Siobhan with a little sigh as she settled herself in her seat.

'Do what?' Kate cast her daughter a sidelong glance.

'Invite them to Copse End,' Siobhan replied. 'Won't we? Mum?' she persisted, when Kate remained silent.

'Of course we will, stupid,' said Connor from the back seat. 'Anyway, Joe has already said he wants to see my console and I've said he can come over when he likes, so that's settled.'

'Mum?' Siobhan's glance was a little fearful now. 'Is that all right?'

'It looks as if it's all arranged,' Kate replied.

'Well, Mr Fielding did buy us that meal…and then to-day…'

'Yes, Siobhan, I know,' said Kate, 'and, believe me, I was thinking the same thing. It's time we returned the hospitality—that's why I've invited them all to lunch next weekend.'

'You've…?' Siobhan gaped at her and then, as what her mother had said fully sank in, she punched the air. 'Yes!' she said, then wriggled down in her seat, pulling the base-ball cap she was wearing over her eyes.

'Mr Fielding, this is Kirsty Austin,' said Kate. Turning to the woman sitting by the side of the bed, she added, 'And this is her mother. Kirsty's in early labour,' she explained as Tom picked up the rather sparse set of notes and flicked through them.

'Hello, Kirsty.' Tom nodded at the girl over the notes. 'Have we seen you in the clinic?'

'No.' The girl sullenly shook her head.

'Was there a reason for that?' asked Tom.

'Yes, I didn't know I was pregnant,' muttered the girl.

'It's been a terrible shock to us all,' said her mother. 'I couldn't believe it. I just thought she was putting on weight, but this…well! I can't imagine what my husband's going to say when he finds out.'

'He doesn't know yet?' asked Kate.

'No.' The woman shook her head. 'He works away—on oil rigs. Goodness knows what he's going to say...'

'How old are you, Kirsty?' Tom sat down on the side of the bed, closer to the girl and with his back half-turned towards her mother.

'Fourteen,' Kirsty replied.

'And I imagine you must have had a pretty trouble-free pregnancy. Am I right?'

'Yes.' She nodded.

'No discomfort at all?' He spoke so gently that, just for a moment, Kate could imagine it was his own daughter he was speaking to. She was reminded of how he had admitted being apprehensive about the forthcoming teenage years, especially where Francesca was concerned, and for the very reason they were witnessing at that moment.

'Well, I didn't get periods,' said the girl. She still spoke sullenly but somehow seemed to be responding to Tom's manner, a mixture of compassion and authority. 'But I sometimes used to miss them anyway so I didn't think anything of it.'

'Anything else?'

'I get a sort of burning feeling here.' She indicated the centre of her chest. 'Usually after I've eaten something.'

'And that's all?'

She nodded.

'What about the baby's father?' asked Tom, his tone as matter-of-fact as if he'd just enquired about the weather.

The girl's gaze flickered to her mother, who gave a sound that was a cross between a sniff and a snort. 'We've yet to establish that,' she stated angrily, 'although it doesn't take much to work it out. Homework in her bedroom, my foot! I don't know how I could have been so stupid!'

'Well, I'm sure Kirsty will tell when she is ready,' said Tom, standing up. 'My only reason for asking is that very often fathers like to be present at the birth of their babies, and if that is the case here, he should be contacted.'

'Over my dead body!' said Kirsty's mother. 'That lout isn't coming anywhere near Kirsty again, I can tell you. Besides, she's underage. He's broken the law.'

'Mrs Austin,' said Kate calmly, intervening, 'Mr Fielding will want to examine Kirsty now, so how about you go and get yourself a nice cup of tea? You can come back and sit with Kirsty again afterwards.'

'What?' Mrs Austin blinked and she looked from one to the other. Then her shoulders seemed to sag and she turned away. 'Oh, all right,' she muttered. Picking up her belongings, she stood up then stalked out of the bay.

'She's upset, Kirsty,' said Kate gently when she saw the girl's lip tremble and tears fill her eyes. 'She'll come round when she sees the baby, you'll see.'

'Right, Kirsty,' said Tom, 'if you'll just let me check that all is well with your baby.' Gently but firmly, and watched by Kate, he examined the girl's abdomen, listened to the baby's heartbeat and finally checked her cervix. 'You've got a little way to go yet,' he said, 'but all is well with your baby. He or she should be with us a little later today. Now, Kirsty, is there anything you want to ask me?'

'What you said just now,' muttered Kirsty, 'about the father being here...?'

'Yes?' Tom raised his eyebrows.

'I would like that.'

'In that case, I would say we really will have to know who he is.' A smile played around Tom's mouth. 'If you like, you can give Sister Ryan the details and she will arrange for him to be contacted. Just one thing, though. Does *he* know? About the baby, I mean?'

'Yes,' Kirsty whispered. 'We sort of guessed a few weeks ago.'

'And yet you didn't see a doctor?'

'No. I thought…well, at first I didn't believe it…and then, well, I didn't realise I was so far on. Then in the night I had some bleeding and some pains and I told my mum. She brought me here this morning…'

'And the father?'

'He's gone to school, I guess. His name is Scott—he lives next door.'

'Right,' said Tom. As Kirsty clutched at her stomach and moaned in pain, he added, 'I'll leave you in Sister Ryan's hands now, but no doubt I'll see you later.' With a smile at Kate he left the antenatal bay.

'You would like Scott here, Kirsty?' asked Kate. When the girl nodded she went on, 'What I suggest is that I bring a phone in here and you can ring the school and ask to speak to him. Maybe we'll tell your mum what you intend doing.'

'She'll go mad,' said Kirsty.

'Nevertheless, she needs to be told. Have you discussed any plans over what is to happen to the baby once it's born?'

'Not really.' Kirsty shook her head. 'There hasn't been time, although when Mum asked what on earth I thought I'd do with a baby and I said that I'd keep it and look after it, she said, no way, that we didn't have room for a baby and that she'd end up looking after it and she wasn't having any more of that—not at her time of life.'

'Well, we'll see what happens after the baby is born,' said Kate. 'Maybe we'll need to involve a social worker to sort things out for you, but first things first. I'm going to get that phone for you, then I'm going to give you an injection to help with the pain and make you a little more comfortable. Now, just try and relax for a while and I'll be back shortly.'

She hurried to the nurses' station where she found Natalie talking to Tom, apparently discussing another case. 'Problems?' she asked, catching sight of Natalie's expression.

'Not unless you call a decided shortage of beds a problem,' Natalie replied.

'We had two spare an hour ago,' said Kate.

'Not any more we don't.' Natalie sighed. 'We've had to admit a threatened miscarriage, which could prove to be a long-term stay, and we have another on her way in—a possible breech delivery. We hadn't bargained on Kirsty, of course,' she added. 'I only hope we don't have another unexpected one otherwise it could be trolleys at dawn in the corridor.'

'Not on my ward it won't,' said Kate with a shudder. 'We'll manage somehow, come what may.'

'I have a meeting to go to,' said Tom, 'but if possible I would like to attend young Kirsty—she's a tiny thing and I fear she may have difficulties delivering naturally. Perhaps you could page me, please, Sister, at the appropriate time?'

'Of course, Mr Fielding,' Kate replied. As he moved away in the direction of his office she picked up a cordless telephone from the desk. 'I'll just take this back to Kirsty,' she said to Natalie, 'make her a bit more comfortable—and placate her mother by the looks of it,' she added as Mrs Austin appeared in the corridor, heading purposefully towards the antenatal suites.

'Rather you than me,' said Natalie with a grin. 'I bet you're wishing you hadn't come in this morning, aren't you?'

'You could say that,' agreed Kate with a sigh. 'Monday mornings are bad enough as it is without all this...'

'Have a good weekend, did you?' asked Natalie.

'Yes, very good actually.' Kate smiled.

'No more tenpin bowling trips with the Fieldings?' From the tone of her voice Natalie was quite obviously joking, but when Kate didn't deny it, as Natalie had apparently expected her to, she threw her a quick, searching glance. 'Kate…?' she said.

'Yes?' Kate raised her eyebrows.

'I said, no more tenpin bowling trips with…?'

'Yes, I know what you said. I heard you.'

'So…?'

Kate sighed. Somehow she couldn't lie, at least not to Natalie. Natalie was her friend. 'Well,' she said, 'not tenpin bowling trips, anyway.'

'Not?' Natalie stared at her. 'You mean there was something else?'

'There might have been.' Kate smiled enigmatically then began to move away from the nurses' station towards the antenatal suites.

'What?' cried Natalie. 'You can't leave it there!'

'Sorry,' called Kate over her shoulder, 'can't stop now—too much to do.'

'But, *Kate*,' Natalie wailed.

'Catch you later!'

'Too right you will,' retorted Natalie.

Chuckling to herself, Kate hurried to the antenatal bay and found Kirsty talking to her mother.

Mrs Austin looked up as Kate approached, holding out the cordless telephone.

'I've told her,' said Kirsty in a small voice, 'about Scott and about how I'd like him to be here.'

'Here's the phone,' said Kate, passing it to the girl.

The look of disgust that had been on Kirsty's mother's face at the first mention of the baby's father had gone now and been replaced by one of if not actual defeat then certainly resignation.

'I think it could be for the best,' said Kate as she drew the curtains around Kirsty's bed to allow the girl some privacy while she made her call. 'Far better that than to alienate her and the boy.'

'What are we going to do?' There was a helpless look in the other woman's eyes now as they moved away from the bed.

'I've suggested to Kirsty that a social worker might be of help while you discuss options,' said Kate. 'You've had a shock, Mrs Austin,' she added kindly, 'and you need time to come to terms with things. Maybe you need to contact your husband and involve him with what has happened.'

'He'll go mad.' The woman shook her head. 'Kirsty is the apple of his eye—his little princess he used to call her. I can't imagine how he'll take this.'

'You may find that he'll be more supportive than you think—once he's got used to the idea, that is.'

'She can't keep the baby. It's out of the question. It'll have to be adopted.'

'At the moment,' said Kate, 'I think Kirsty is saying that she does want to keep the baby. What you need to think about, Mrs Austin, is that this baby will be your grandchild, yours and your husband's. Maybe he won't want his grandchild being adopted by strangers. And then, of course, there is Scott and his family...'

'The Armstrongs?' Mrs Austin looked up sharply as if this aspect of events hadn't occurred to her. 'They are our next-door neighbours! Oh, lord, what a mess all this is!'

'The most important thing at the moment,' said Kate gently, 'is to get Kirsty and Scott's baby safely delivered, and that's my job. Now, I'm going to give Kirsty an injection to help with the pain. You can sit with her if you wish

but I don't think it's a good idea at this stage to worry her
with the moral aspect of what has happened or the practi-
calities of what is to happen in the future. There will be
time enough for all that later. I suggest that all Kirsty needs
at the moment is love and support, especially from her
mum.'

'She's only fourteen, Sister…' said Mrs Austin helplessly.

'Yes, I know,' Kate replied patiently. 'Now, come on,'
she went on after a moment, 'she'll be wondering where
you are.' Briskly she led the way back to Kirsty's bed and
after checking that the girl had finished her telephone conversation she drew back the curtains. 'Did you speak to
Scott?' she asked.

'Yes.' Kirsty nodded. 'He says he's coming in—and he's
going to tell his parents.'

'Well, that's a start anyway,' said Kate with a glance at
Kirsty's mother. 'He has responsibilities now and at least
he's started to face up to them. Now, Kirsty, I have something here to help with the pain.' Turning the girl onto her
side, Kate swabbed the skin on her upper thigh and swiftly
administered an intramuscular analgesic.

Leaving mother and daughter together, Kate made her
way back to the nurses' station, which by this time was a
frantic hive of activity. The threatened miscarriage case had
arrived and was being admitted; two babies had been delivered in the labour suites, and the new fathers, still in a
state of shock, were trying to phone their families; a woman
attending an antenatal clinic had gone into premature labour
and because of the shortage of beds had been placed in one
of the postnatal suites; and if all that wasn't enough, the
phone on the desk was ringing and when Kate took the call
it was from a paramedic to say that a woman had just given

birth in the back of an ambulance and they would be arriving at the hospital in the next ten minutes.

'We'll need a paediatrician on hand for the baby and an obstetrician to check the mother,' the paramedic went on to explain.

'Are there any specific problems?' asked Kate, at the same time frantically wondering where she would put the new arrivals.

'Baby is having difficulties with his breathing and mother is bleeding profusely—we've set up an infusion but both of them will need urgent attention.'

'Right, thank you,' Kate replied. 'We'll be ready.' Lifting her phone again, she dialled the number for Tom's pager. He answered almost immediately. 'Mr Fielding,' she said. 'Sister Ryan here.'

'Hello, Kate,' he said, and for some inexplicable reason her heart turned over. She couldn't imagine why, then quickly came to the conclusion that it was because in all the bustle and confusion she had momentarily forgotten the weekend and all that had happened—the shared intimacies, the laughter and the companionship. She had been expecting a formal greeting from Tom, 'Sister Ryan' instead of simply 'Kate'.

'We have an emergency coming in,' she finally managed to say. 'Baby delivered by paramedics, mother apparently suffering a postpartum haemorrhage. Arrival expected in about ten minutes.'

'I'll come down,' Tom replied. 'Neil Richardson is about to go into Theatre but Matt Forrester is here. I'll ask him to come with me if you like.'

'Thank you, Mr Fielding,' she replied. 'Sorry to have interrupted your meeting.'

'That's OK. It had almost finished anyway.'

As Kate replaced the receiver Melissa came out of the

antenatal suite. 'Kirsty is in fairly strong labour now,' she said.

'I'll come and see her,' said Kate. 'It's probably time we moved her into the labour suite.' She was about to move away from the desk when she caught sight of a boy who had just come through the double doors onto the unit. With his fresh complexion and gelled hair, he reminded Kate of Joe Fielding. An older man, whom she assumed to be his father, accompanied him. 'Ah,' she said, 'it looks like someone else has come to see Kirsty.' She moved forward to meet the pair who looked as if they were in a state of shock. 'Can I help you?' she said. 'I'm Sister Ryan.'

'My name's Sam Armstrong,' said the older man, 'and this is my son, Scott. The school called me to say…' He trailed off seemingly struggling to find the right words.

'Hello, Mr Armstrong, hello, Scott,' said Kate pleasantly. 'You'll be here to see Kirsty, Scott,' she added, 'and there's no doubt she'll be pleased to see you. Now, Mr Armstrong, if you'd like to wait over there in the relatives' room. Scott, if you would come with me.'

Sam Armstrong seemed quite relieved to be going to the relatives' room. As Scott followed Kate to the antenatal suite she turned and spoke to him. 'Kirsty is in labour, Scott, and you can sit with her for as long as you want to.'

'What about when the baby's born?' His face was deathly pale and he looked terrified. For a moment Kate felt sorry for him.

'Well, we'll see about that when the time comes,' she said. 'But you can certainly help by comforting Kirsty at this stage.'

'Is…is…her mother there?' asked Scott fearfully.

'Yes, Scott, she is,' Kate replied, then was forced to smother a smile as Scott swore under his breath.

When they entered the antenatal suite and approached

Kirsty's bed, Mrs Austin's reaction to seeing Scott was somehow lost in Kirsty's overwhelming joy and relief.

'I would say there's real love there between those two, young as they are,' said Kate to Mary as she returned to the nurses' station a few moments later.

'It's the boy's father I feel sorry for,' said Mary, as Kirsty's mother stalked out of the antenatal suite and headed for the relatives' room. 'That's what you call falling out with the neighbours—big time.'

'You never know,' said Kate, 'it could just all turn out for the best.'

'You mean one big happy family all doting on one small baby?'

'Something like that.' Kate smiled. 'Stranger things have happened. Now, Mary, what next?'

'Gillian Edgerton is about to deliver—Natalie is with her. And Mr Fielding has just arrived to examine the lady who delivered in the ambulance. Oh, looks like they are here now...' Mary broke off as the paramedics came through the double doors to the unit with their patient on a stretcher.

'Morning, Sister,' said the younger of the paramedics cheerfully.

'Good morning, Paul.' Together with Mary, Kate hurried forward.

'This is Mrs Perren,' the paramedic said. 'Dee Perren. She gave us all a surprise this morning when she gave birth to little Timothy in the back of our ambulance. Isn't that right, Dee?'

The woman nodded. She looked exhausted and very pale. 'I want my baby,' she whispered.

'Of course you do,' said Kate as she checked the infusion the paramedics had set up. 'He will be down in the special care baby unit by now, where he will be very well looked after by Sister Forrester and her team. What we have to do is to get you ready so that you can go and see him.'

The next few minutes were a flurry of activity as Dee Perren was transferred to a bed—it had to be in the labour suite as there were no antenatal beds available—the paramedics departed and Tom came to examine Dee.

'The placenta has broken and parts have been retained in the uterus,' Tom said to Kate after his examination. 'We need to get her straight to Theatre for a D and C. If you'll have her prepped, please, Sister, while I scrub up.'

'Certainly, Mr Fielding.' They were professionals again, not friends, as the busy ward routine went on. Kirsty Austin, by this time in strong labour, was moved to the labour suite and Dee Perren was prepared for Theatre.

'I'm scared, Sister,' said Dee fearfully, clinging to Kate's hand as she accompanied her to the anaesthetics room.

'Don't be,' said Kate gently. 'It'll soon be over.'

'What are they going to do? I know the surgeon told me but I can't remember what he said.'

'You'll have an injection in the back of your hand to put you to sleep,' Kate explained, 'then when you are in Theatre Mr Fielding will clear your womb of all the bits of the afterbirth that have been left behind and he'll cauterise it to stop the bleeding. You'll also be given a blood transfusion to replace the blood you've lost.'

'And after that I'll be able to see my baby?' Dee asked tearfully.

'Yes, of course,' Kate replied. 'And we've had another call from your husband to say he's on his way, so by the time you wake up, he'll probably be here.'

'Will you stay with me until I'm asleep?'

'Of course I will.' With a reassuring smile Kate guided the trolley into the anaesthetics room.

When Dee was unconscious and had been taken into

Theatre, Kate returned to the nurses' station where she escorted a new mother and her baby to the postnatal suite. On her return Mary reported that Kirsty seemed to be in difficulties. 'She's had gas and air but she's exhausted,' she said. 'I don't think she's going to be able to push much longer.'

'I'll take a look at her,' said Kate, and together she and Mary made their way to the labour suite.

'You need a bit of help, Kirsty,' she said after she'd examined the girl. 'We're going to use some forceps to deliver your baby. I suggest, Scott...' she turned to the boy, who was sitting beside the bed '...you go to the relatives' room and wait.' Kate smothered a smile as Scott fled at the mention of forceps and delivery.

By this time Tom was out of Theatre and when Kate paged him he came immediately to attend Kirsty. Gently and quietly he talked to the frightened and exhausted girl, reassuring her as he administered a local anaesthetic and performed a small incision before using forceps to help ease her baby into the world.

'We have a girl,' he said a little later. In the moment after he'd cut the cord and with the baby still in his hands, his gaze briefly met Kate's and in that instant she knew that they were both thinking of their own daughters—of how they had once been the size of the baby that had just been delivered, and of how they were both now nearly the same age as the baby's young mother. A moment later Tom gently placed the baby in Kirsty's arms and both he and Kate witnessed the look of awe and amazement on the girl's face as that which until very recently she had chosen to deny became reality.

'Hello, little baby,' she whispered. 'Hello, Lucy.' As the baby's face crumpled, she said, 'Don't cry—Mummy's here.'

It was Tom himself who, a little later and accompanied by Kate, went to the relatives' room where they were greeted by three anxious faces. 'All is well,' he said. Looking directly at Scott, he added, 'Congratulations, you have a healthy daughter.'

Scott flushed scarlet, his father gave a huge sigh of relief and Kirsty's mother promptly burst into tears.

'If you'd like to come with me,' said Kate, 'I'll take you down to the postnatal ward to see Kirsty and the baby.'

They found Kirsty sitting up in bed, still a little dazed from the birth, with the baby in her arms and Melissa by her side. 'Look, Scott,' she said, lifting back the shawl so that he could see the baby's tiny face and a tuft of dark hair. 'Isn't she beautiful?'

Kate and Tom left Scott and Kirsty and their daughter, and Mrs Austin and Sam Armstrong admiring their new granddaughter, and made their way back to the nurses' station.

'You were thinking what I was thinking back there, weren't you?' said Tom as they walked down the corridor.

'If you mean that Siobhan and Francesca aren't far off that girl's age, yes,' she admitted.

'And Joe,' he said.

'Yes,' she agreed, 'and Joe.'

'That boy probably is the same age as Joe and now he's a father—it's a very sobering thought,' Tom added.

Natalie was seated behind the desk at the nurses' station and she looked up as they approached, her eyes narrowing slightly as she saw them together apparently deep in conversation. 'David Perren has just arrived,' she said, looking from one to the other. 'Is his wife ready to go down to SCBU yet?'

'Yes, she can go.' Kate nodded. 'Melissa can go down with her. Perhaps you'd like to page a porter, Natalie.'

'Do you think it would be safe for me to go and take a clinic?' asked Tom with a sigh.

'Well, you could try, Mr Fielding,' said Kate with a smile, 'but don't be surprised if I have to call you back in the middle of it. It appears to be one of those days.'

'For you, Sister—anything.' Tom smiled, one of the rare smiles that lit up his whole face—something that wasn't too familiar with the staff but which Kate had now witnessed several times.

'Friendly today, isn't he?' murmured Natalie as Tom disappeared down the corridor. 'Perhaps he had a good weekend. Speaking of which…' She turned to Kate, but Kate, anticipating her next question, had moved briskly away, picking up a pile of folders and retreating to her office where she closed the door firmly behind her.

She knew, however, there could be no avoiding Natalie for ever, just as she knew that once Natalie got her teeth into something she wasn't inclined to let go until she had all the details. The moment came at the end of the shift as Kate was walking to the car park. Hearing a shout, she turned and saw Natalie running to catch her up.

Fully expecting her friend to launch into a full-scale interrogation, she braced herself.

'I've just been talking to Michelle Steane from Special Care,' said Natalie, and Kate relaxed a little. 'Apparently little Timothy Perren is in trouble.'

'Oh, no!' Kate frowned. 'Dee was so happy when she went down to see him. What's the problem, did Michelle say?'

'Respiratory problems apparently,' Natalie replied. 'Serious enough for them to call Reverend Collard in to baptise him.'

'Oh, I hope he pulls through,' said Kate. 'Poor little love, he's had enough drama in his life already, what with making his debut in the back of an ambulance.'

'Well, he has a first-class team looking after him down there on SCBU—just like his mum had on Matty,' said Natalie. As they reached their cars, which were parked alongside each other, she said, 'So, are you going to tell me or not?'

'Tell you what?' Kate smiled.

'You know what,' Natalie retorted. 'You saw Tom Fielding again at the weekend, didn't you?'

'You make it sound like a date!' protested Kate.

'Well, it might have been,' said Natalie. 'You're being evasive enough about it.'

'I can assure you it wasn't a date.' Kate hesitated, wondering just how much she should tell Natalie, for although she was a good friend she did go overboard rather if she thought there was a chance at matchmaking.

'So what was it? Go on, tell me, otherwise I really will start to think there was more to it.'

'He phoned,' Kate said, trying to make it sound as casual as possible, which of course it was. It was only someone like Natalie who could possibly read anything into it. 'On Saturday morning.'

'Really?' Natalie was obviously intrigued. 'Go on.'

'He invited us—me and the children—over to his house.'

'To lunch, you mean?'

'Sort of.' Kate nodded. 'He said he was going to barbeque some food and he wondered if the children would like to use his pool. It was so hot on Saturday and—'

'His *pool*!' Natalie stared at her. 'He has a *swimming pool*?'

'Well, yes…'

'Where does he live? What's his house like?'

'He lives over at Lower Melbury and his house is very

nice,' Kate replied patiently. 'We had a lovely time and the kids all enjoyed themselves. Now, if you don't mind, Nat, I really must get on. I have shopping to do before I go home.'

Somehow she got away but from the expression on Natalie's face she knew the subject was far from closed and would be brought up again at the slightest opportunity. As she drove away she couldn't help but wonder what her friend would make of the fact that she had invited Tom and his family to lunch the following weekend.

CHAPTER FIVE

KATE found herself in an agony of indecision as the weekend approached. It had started as far back as Tuesday or Wednesday when she had tried to decide on the nature of the meal they were to have. She had said lunch, but with young, hungry mouths to feed should that be a formal sort of sit-down lunch, maybe a roast with all the trimmings or should she settle for a buffet-style lunch? The latter would certainly be more relaxed and would probably appeal to the children but, on the other hand, would that be what Tom would like? In the end it was a suggestion of Aunt Bessie's that held the most appeal.

'Given that the weather will last, which according to the long-range forecasts it should, why not set up the old trestle table in the garden under the apple trees?' she said in her down-to-earth manner. 'There will easily be enough room to seat everyone and you could serve a hot dish with a selection of salads.'

'Aunt Bessie.' Kate stared at her. 'That's a wonderful idea. I could make lasagne…'

'And I'll make apple and cherry pies for afters.'

'That would be marvellous, and you will, of course, join us.'

'Well, I don't know about that,' Aunt Bessie began dubiously.

'Oh, please,' said Kate. 'I want to know what you think of our new friends and, besides, I need you there for moral support.'

'Well, if you put it like that…'

So that was the food decided and by Friday Kate had also done the shopping and Aunt Bessie had made her pies. All that remained now was the weather and what to wear. In recent times Kate had been given to grabbing the first thing that had come to hand but when, to her relief, Saturday morning dawned with a light mist that hung over the garden and the copse beyond, and with more than a hint of the warmth that was to come, she found herself critically surveying her wardrobe, discarding the white trousers and T-shirt she had planned to wear but wondering frantically what on earth she could wear instead. She had bought hardly any clothes for herself since Liam had died and some of her dresses she'd had for at least four or even five years. Not that Tom would know that, of course, because he wouldn't have seen her in any of them. Not that that should matter, she told herself firmly. After all, it wasn't as if this lunch was a date—it was simply the sharing of a family meal, the returning of hospitality.

In spite of that, she still found herself trying on a couple of dresses and discarding them before settling on an ankle-length, sleeveless dress in a brightly coloured Aztec design which was a perfect contrast to her dark hair. She added some chunky jewellery and was just stepping into a pair of gold sandals when Siobhan stuck her head round the bedroom door.

'Mum…' she began, then stopped when she caught sight of Kate and stared at her. 'You haven't worn that dress for…ages,' she said.

'No, I haven't,' Kate agreed, hoping that her daughter wasn't going to start reminiscing over exactly when she had last worn it. She wasn't sure she could cope with that. Not today. 'Does it look all right?' she asked as casually as she could, not wanting Siobhan to know how much effort she had put into her appearance.

'Yes.' Siobhan nodded. 'It looks fab. What about this?' She looked down at her own clothes. 'Will this be all right? I didn't know what to wear.'

Kate's breath caught in her throat as she realised that her daughter had probably suffered as many agonies as herself, that she was growing up fast and that it was terribly important to her that she also should wear the right thing, especially with Francesca coming and, probably more importantly, Joe. She'd chosen a turquoise peasant-style off-the-shoulder top and a pair of cropped trousers. 'Yes, darling, you look lovely.'

'I wish my hair wasn't so wild and curly and so…so… red,' muttered Siobhan.

'But, darling, that's you,' protested Kate. 'It's what makes you special…different.'

'I don't want to be different. Why can't I have dark hair like you…like Francesca?' she demanded moodily.

'Because you have Daddy's colouring, that's why— aren't you proud about that?'

'Yes…yes…I s'ppose.'

'Well, there you are, then.'

'But it was different then, when Daddy was here. People could see I was like him, that I had his colour hair. Now it's just me…and with people who didn't know Daddy it's hard to explain…'

'You don't have to explain anything, darling,' said Kate gently. 'Now, we must get on, they'll be here before we know where we are. Come and help me with the salads.'

It had a continental feel about it—the long trestle table set up beneath the trees and the slightly unnatural heat they were enjoying, and any anxieties they may have had about the suitability of the arrangements were quickly swept away when Tom arrived with Joe and Francesca and the pleasure on their faces was apparent.

Tom, in cream chinos and T-shirt, came bearing wine
and flowers, some for Kate and some for Aunt Bessie who
was immediately captivated by his quiet manner and easy
charm. Siobhan and Connor, after only a moment's shy-
ness, bore Joe and Francesca away to explore the house
and the garden.

'This is wonderful,' said Tom, leaning back in a deck-
chair, a glass of wine in his hand. 'It reminds me of the
house I was brought up in. I'm sure if I really listened I
could hear the sound of a tennis ball against a racket.'

'We don't have a tennis court, I'm afraid,' said Kate with
a laugh, 'but, yes, you're right, it is a lovely old house.'

'Do you know, Dad,' said Francesca, her dark eyes dancing with excitement, when Kate called everyone for lunch,
'they have their very own wood? Down there at the bottom
of the garden!'

'It's just a copse really,' said Kate, her gaze meeting
Tom's.

'You'll have to show me later,' he said.

For some absurd reason the thought of that, of showing
Tom the copse, stayed with her throughout lunch, almost
like she'd felt as a child when there had been something
exciting to look forward to.

Lunch was a tremendous success—Kate's lasagne,
served with crusty bread and every conceivable type of
salad, followed by Aunt Bessie's mouth-watering apple and
cherry pies and lashings of fresh cream, all washed down
with red wine or home-made lemonade.

Afterwards Aunt Bessie made her excuses and took herself off indoors for a nap while the children disappeared
upstairs on their own, leaving Tom and Kate alone.

'I feel lazy now,' he said, leaning back and linking his
hands behind his head.

'So you should,' she said. 'It is the weekend after all.'

'That was a wonderful meal,' he said with a sigh. 'And as for Aunt Bessie, well, she's quite simply a treasure, isn't she?'

'Yes, she is,' Kate agreed with a little smile. 'We are so lucky to have her.'

They were silent for a while, completely at ease in each other's company. The only sounds in the garden were the song of a blackbird in the branches of the apple trees above them and the distant hum of a neighbour's lawnmower. Kate could still hardly believe how comfortable she felt in Tom's company and how, if anyone had told her only a month or so ago that they would be sitting like this under the apple trees in the garden, she would never have believed them.

'How about,' Tom said at last, breaking the silence between them, 'you show me this copse of yours?'

Her heart leapt. Why, she had no idea save for the fact that this was what had been at the back of her mind ever since he'd mentioned it—what, almost unconsciously, she had been looking forward to.

'Yes, all right,' she said, she hoped casually, without giving away anything of her feelings, which, when she really examined them, were ridiculous. This, after all, was merely a stroll with a man who, in spite of what they had shared recently, was still her boss. And even if he weren't, she told herself firmly as they stood up and began to stroll down the crazy paving between the masses of cottage-garden flowers—the marguerites, lavender, delphiniums and hollyhocks—this would be nothing to get excited about. That sort of excitement had gone for her, had died along with Liam and was never likely to be repeated.

So, if that was the case, what was this she was feeling? This little frisson of anticipation that had remained with her throughout the meal and was still there now as they left the flowers behind and approached the copse, their feet making no sound on the thick, mossy ground.

It was cool in the copse, the hot sun filtering through the trees and forming dappled patches on the ground.

'Does this really belong to the house?' asked Tom as they walked side by side. 'Or is it part of common ground?'

'No,' Kate replied, 'it really is part of Copse End. My great-uncle—Aunt Bessie's late husband—inherited the property from his father. I understand it had been in his family for some years.'

'Well, it really is delightful, and quite unique these days.'

'It's beautiful in the spring when the bluebells are out,' said Kate as they paused for a moment and looked around.

'Where did you live before?' he asked after a while, when they carried on walking.

'In a three-bedroomed semi on the other side of Franchester,' she replied. 'It was pleasant and fairly quiet— but nothing like this.'

They walked on in companionable silence then Tom spoke. 'We nearly didn't make it today,' he said, and Kate had the sudden but distinct impression that he had been struggling to decide whether he should tell her that or not. They had reached the end of the copse by then, and the fence and gate which marked the boundary. They stopped and leaned over the gate, looking out over the adjoining fields of crops.

'Should I ask why?' she enquired, turning her head to look at him.

'Jennifer,' he said.

'Ah,' she replied, then, when he remained silent, continued casually, 'Do you want to tell me about it?'

'I suppose there's not a lot to tell really, but I found it...irritating.' He was silent again for a long moment, as if by talking about his ex-wife he was somehow breaking the habit of a lifetime. Then, as if once more reaching a decision, he said, 'It wasn't really my weekend to have Joe and Francesca, so after your invitation I spoke to Jennifer last Sunday and asked if she would mind them coming to me today.'

'Surely she didn't object to that?' Kate stared at him.

'No, of course she didn't,' he said quickly, 'at least not at the time. But then she phoned, late last night actually, and said they had some friends coming today and that she'd particularly like the children there—to meet these friends, she said.'

'What did you say?' Suddenly Kate was curious.

'I told her that arrangements had already been made and it would be discourteous to change them.'

'Did she accept that?'

'She argued and said surely an excuse could be found. I told her I didn't want to make an excuse and that I felt sure the children wouldn't want to either.'

'What happened then?'

'She argued a bit more. She thought I would give in, as I must admit I usually do when it's anything to do with the children, but this time I didn't. She hung up on me in the end.'

'Did she bring Joe and Francesca over to you this morning?'

Tom shook his head. 'No, I went and picked them up— I didn't see Jennifer.'

'Did the children say anything?' Kate bit her lip. The last thing she wanted was to have been the cause of any friction for Tom and his children.

'No, not really. They were very quiet actually, although I wasn't in any doubt that they wanted to come here.'

They were silent again for a while, watching a tractor in the distance as it trundled across a field. 'When you first spoke to Jennifer, did you tell her where you wanted to go?' asked Kate at last.

'No.' Tom shook his head. 'I simply said a friend had invited us to lunch, but I gather that in the meantime Francesca had filled her in on the details—which, of course, I quite understand. I have no problem with that.'

'It sounds, though, as if Jennifer did,' said Kate quietly.

'I can't see why,' he began. 'After all, she has exactly what she wants.'

'She's a woman,' said Kate philosophically.

'But she's known when I've taken other women out. In fact, in one case she actually encouraged me to go out with one of her friends...'

'And did you?'

'Yes.' He nodded.

'And?'

'It was a complete and utter disaster,' he admitted. 'But that's beside the point. I still don't see why she had to be difficult over this.'

'I'm an unknown entity,' said Kate. '*She* doesn't know I'm simply a colleague of yours. But, quite apart from that, this time her children are involved.'

'They are my children as well,' said Tom. He turned his head to look at her and added, 'Is that how you see this?'

'See what?' Kate frowned.

'This...friendship. Do you see it that we are only colleagues, or keeping it going for the sake of the children?'

'Isn't that how *you* see it?' she asked, and as she spoke she allowed her gaze to meet his.

'At first...perhaps,' he said. 'Now I'm not so sure.' Lifting his hand, he reached out and very gently ran the backs of his fingers down the side of her cheek.

At his touch Kate froze. This was the first time a man had touched her since Liam, not counting that obnoxious man from Admin whom she'd long chosen to forget, and this was nothing like that. This was gentle, tender even, and stirred the echo of some long-forgotten desire that had lain buried deep inside her.

There was no telling what might have happened next if they had remained there, alone and undisturbed. Maybe Tom would have drawn her into his arms, maybe he would have kissed her—there was no knowing. Neither was there any knowing what her reaction might have been because at that moment they heard a shout in the copse behind them, followed by the sound of laughter, and seconds later Siobhan and Francesca erupted from the trees.

'Have you seen the boys?' demanded Siobhan.

'No.' It was Kate who replied, rather shakily in the event. She hoped her daughter wouldn't notice anything untoward. 'Have you lost them?'

'They went off to hide,' said Francesca breathlessly. 'They said we wouldn't be able to find them, we said we would.'

'In that case,' said Tom, 'perhaps you'd better keep trying. They certainly haven't come this way.'

The girls turned and scurried back the way they had come and Kate and Tom were alone again, but the moment had gone, that moment of magic, which could so easily have turned into one of intimacy, had passed, leaving Kate, at least, feeling a little foolish. 'We'd better go back,' she said.

'Yes,' Tom agreed, and just for a moment Kate thought she detected a note of reluctance in his voice. 'It's getting late and I said I'd get Joe and Francesca back to their mother between five and six o'clock.'

'He's a lovely man,' said Aunt Bessie. It was much later. Tom, Joe and Francesca had gone, and Kate and Aunt Bessie were clearing up.

'Yes,' Kate agreed, 'he is nice and his children are great, too.'

'He seems rather fond of you, Kate,' Aunt Bessie observed as she wiped down the kitchen worktops.

'We've known each other a long time—he's a good colleague,' said Kate warily.

'I thought it seemed a bit more than that,' her aunt replied bluntly. Aunt Bessie was never one for mincing her words.

'No.' Kate shook her head. 'It's nothing like that.'

'I don't see why not. He's divorced, isn't he?'

'Well, yes, although it seems his ex-wife appears a bit reluctant for him to move on in his life.'

'Hasn't she remarried?' Aunt Bessie paused and peered at Kate over the top of her glasses.

'Yes, she has.'

'Then she can hardly have any say in what her ex-husband does, can she?'

'No, I suppose not.'

'Whom did she marry?'

'Her childhood sweetheart apparently. Tom says she should have married him in the first place and saved everyone a lot of heartache.'

'He's probably right,' said Aunt Bessie grimly. 'It sounds to me as if she wants to have her cake and eat it. In my experience people like her soon find out that life isn't like that.' She paused and the silence was heavy with unspoken words. Then, looking at Kate, she said, 'Do you not think it might be time for you to move on a bit, Kate?'

'No,' said Kate quickly, 'no. I don't think so, not yet. Liam…'

'Liam is dead, Kate,' said Aunt Bessie gently. 'I'm sorry

to be so blunt, but it's a fact. He was your husband and the father of your children and you vowed to love him with all your heart, but you were released from that vow with Liam's death.'

'I know,' said Kate, 'I know…but…'

'You are still young, Kate, and you have the rest of your life before you. I would hate to think you would spend that life alone, and I happen to know for a fact that Liam wouldn't have wanted you to.'

'How do you know that?' Her eyes swimming with sudden, unshed tears, Kate looked at Aunt Bessie.

'Because he told me so,' she replied.

'But he couldn't have known…'

'No, he couldn't have known he was going to lose his life so tragically and so soon, but he was a policeman, Kate, and he knew it might happen to him. We spoke of it once and he told me that if it did happen while you were still young, he hoped you could find happiness with someone else.'

'Liam said that?' The tears ran down Kate's cheeks now and she dashed them away with her hand.

'Yes, Kate, he did. Now, I'm not suggesting you go off deliberately looking for someone, because it rarely happens that way. When it does happen it's usually totally unexpected and quite often with someone who's been there right under your nose for a very long time.'

'You're talking about Tom Fielding again,' said Kate with a watery smile.

'It may be him, it may not,' Aunt Bessie replied, 'but what I am saying is that you shouldn't close your heart or your mind to the possibility. You owe it to yourself and to the children, and as a compliment to Liam, to show the world that you can be happy again.

* * *

Kate thought long and hard that night about what Aunt Bessie had said and eventually came to the conclusion that as usual it was full of her aunt's common sense and down-to-earth wisdom.

Maybe it *was* time to move on, to put her life back together again. Maybe it was what Liam would have wanted, and maybe there was someone out there who would be right for her. But was Tom Fielding the one? Aunt Bessie had hinted at it and Natalie was constantly trying to read more into the situation than was actually there. But how did she herself feel about him? she asked herself as she prepared for bed. She liked him but, then, she'd always liked him, he'd been around at work for a very long time—but wasn't that just what Aunt Bessie had implied, that when it happened, more often than not it would be with someone like that, someone who was right there?

But things had changed in the last couple of weeks because it wasn't now just a case of Tom being right there, at work each day. Now there were outings and meals, and today there had been something else, something elusive, almost intangible but at the same time, nevertheless, very real. It had started with that little frisson of anticipation over her showing him the copse—silly really but, again, very real. And then during their walk there had been that heart-stopping moment when he had touched her. The incident itself had been so slight, so slender that to anyone else it might have seemed inconsequential, but somehow, to Kate, it had been a moment that could signify a change in their relationship, a moment that could determine whether they stopped right there or whether they moved forward.

But what of Tom? Did he want more? Did he want their relationship to move forward? He'd left without making any further plans but that could have been because they had left it late before leaving. On the other hand, maybe he'd decided not to pursue the relationship any further. He'd already told her he found it difficult to trust a woman again—would he be unable to trust her? Or did he simply feel the situation could become too complicated, what with his children and her children, with Aunt Bessie, his ex-wife and, last but by no means least, the fact that they worked together—which in itself could be a recipe for disaster?

On the other hand, she thought as she stepped into the shower, maybe the truth was far simpler than all that. Perhaps he just didn't find her attractive: end of story. After all, she wasn't exactly in the first flush of youth and she *had* had two children.

It was with that sobering thought uppermost in her mind that a little later she stepped out of the shower, wrapped herself in a towel and wound another round her head before padding into her bedroom, only to find that the phone on her bedside table was ringing. Leaning across the bed, she lifted the receiver. 'Hello?' she said, wondering who could be ringing her so late.

'Kate?'

There was no mistaking the voice and she felt her heart give a delicious little flutter. 'Tom?' she said.

'I'm sorry to be ringing so late,' he said. 'Did I wake you? I was about to hang up.'

'No,' she said quickly, 'nothing like that. I was in the shower.'

'So are you now dripping water all over the sitting-room floor?'

'No.' She laughed. 'It's all right. I'm in the bedroom. I have a phone by the bed and I'm well wrapped up in towels.'

'I see,' he said, and to Kate, listening, it was as if he was contemplating the thought of her wrapped in towels and lying on her bed. 'I just wanted to apologise for rushing away the way we did.'

'Oh, that's all right,' she said. 'You were late. I hadn't realised the time had gone so quickly.'

'Yes, well, normally I wouldn't have worried but—'

'Jennifer wanted the children back, I know.'

'No,' he interrupted her, 'I wasn't going to say that. I was going to say that Joe gets anxious if he's late for anything.'

'So were you late?' she asked.

'Not really. The friends Jennifer had wanted the children to see were still there—at least, there was a strange car on the drive so I assume it was them.'

'Did you see Jennifer?' she asked. She didn't know why she'd said it—really, it was none of her business—but suddenly, for some obscure reason which she was at a loss to work out, she needed to know.

'No,' he said, 'she didn't come out. He did—Max Oliver—and the children went inside with him.'

'It must be very hard for you,' she said, 'seeing your children with another man.'

'It was at first,' he admitted, 'but I've got used to it now. But that's beside the point. Apart from apologising for rushing off, I also wanted to say how much we all enjoyed today and to thank you for everything.'

'That's all right,' said Kate. She spoke casually but nevertheless she was pleased. 'We enjoyed it, too.'

'Thank Bessie for us as well, won't you?'

'I will.'

'She's a delightful lady,' he said.

Kate laughed. 'You two could set up a mutual admiration society,' she said. 'She's been singing your praises as well.'

'Oh?' He sounded interested. 'Are you saying she approved of me?'

'Oh, definitely.'

'So could that mean that by getting past Aunt Bessie I could be in with a chance?' he said. There was a hint of amusement in his voice but Kate found herself gripping the receiver a little more tightly.

'It depends,' she replied lightly, 'on what your intentions are.'

'Well,' he said slowly, as if considering carefully, 'I was wondering if we might make another arrangement.'

'I don't see why not,' she replied. 'What did you have in mind? Tenpin bowling again? Or how about a picnic somewhere? We could perhaps meet you all…'

'Actually, Kate, no,' he said, and his tone of voice had changed now, losing that hint of amusement and taking on a serious note. 'That wasn't what I had in mind this time.'

'Oh?' she said. 'Don't you like picnics? I thought perhaps we could go to the beach…'

'Yes,' he said, 'I do like picnics, so do Joe and Francesca, and the beach sounds a wonderful idea, but maybe another time. What I had in mind was that just you and I go somewhere.'

'Oh!' she said, and her breath caught in her throat.

'Would Bessie keep an eye on Siobhan and Connor?'

'Yes,' she replied, trying to ignore the little knot of excitement that was there again in the pit of her stomach, just like it had been earlier in the day. 'Yes, I'm sure she would.'

'Well, in that case, how about next Friday? I can pick you up and we can go somewhere for a quiet meal—just the two of us.'

'Yes, Tom,' she heard herself say. 'I would like that.'

'That's settled, then.' He sounded pleased. 'I'd better go now and let you get some sleep. I'll see you on Monday, Kate. Goodnight.'

'Goodnight.' She replaced the receiver then rolled over onto her back and gazed up at the ceiling. She had a date. She was actually going out with another man, and if that tingle of excitement had been anything to go by she knew that she would be counting the days until Friday.

But as the excitement subsided a little Kate knew she couldn't get away from the fact that the man who was causing this excitement was still her boss, with all the pitfalls that situation implied. She made up her mind, there and then, that her professional relationship with him would have to be kept distinctly separate from her private one.

CHAPTER SIX

'SISTER!'

Kate was on her way to her office but paused as she heard the call from a bed in the antenatal bay. She walked back. Its occupant, Sara Millington, was a petite girl in her early twenties with long hair and huge brown eyes, who had been admitted with high blood pressure two days previously and who was thirty-eight weeks into her pregnancy. 'What is it, Sara?' she asked, frowning when she saw the girl's ashen appearance. 'Is there something wrong?'

'That woman,' whispered Sara, her eyes enormous as she stared towards the nurses' station.

'What woman?'

'The one the ambulancemen have just brought in.'

'What about her?'

'I know her,' said Sara.

'Well, that often happens in here,' said Kate, preparing to move on. It was the start of what promised to be a busy day and she had no time to stand talking.

'No.' Sara was shaking her head. 'You don't understand. I...I...I have to talk to you, Sister.' She looked up at Kate, her expression one of helpless despair.

Kate hesitated. Her workload was awesome but at the same time she knew that Tom planned to induce Sara's labour that morning, and he would be less than pleased if she was being placed under any undue stress that might raise her blood pressure even more. With a quick flick of her wrist Kate drew the curtains around the girl's bed and sat down on a chair beside her. 'So, tell me,' she said. 'What is this all about?'

'Well,' gulped Sara, 'you know Philip, my boyfriend?'

'Was that him who visited you yesterday?' asked Kate.

'Yes.' Sara nodded and Kate noticed that her eyes had filled with tears. 'Well, that woman…that's just come in…'

'What about her?'

'She's…she's his wife!'

'His wife?' Kate stared at her. She was well used to these situations on Maternity but somehow found herself a little surprised at this particular triangle. She'd had Sara and her boyfriend down as a devoted young couple, eagerly awaiting the arrival of their first baby and no doubt planning their wedding and their future life together.

'Yes, but…why is she in here? I don't understand,' Sara went on. 'If she's in here she must be having a baby and Philip said…well, he said they hadn't slept together for a very long time. He is on the point of leaving her to be with me…and our baby,' she explained earnestly.

'Does his wife know about you?' asked Kate quietly.

'Yes.' Sara nodded. 'She found out some time ago. Philip and I work together, you see. She told him he had to end our affair but…he couldn't, especially after we found that I was pregnant.'

'Does she know any of this—about the baby or that the affair has continued?'

Sara shook her head. 'No, he was going to tell her,' she whispered. 'He said as soon as our baby was born…then he would leave her and move into my flat with me. He loves me,' she said almost pleadingly, desperate now for Kate to understand the situation.

'I'm sure he does,' said Kate, forcing herself to remain neutral.

'But she's pregnant!' Sara shook her head. 'How can she

be, when they don't even sleep together? Philip told me that she wouldn't forgive him for his affair with me and he has been sleeping in the spare room. He said he didn't mind that because he didn't want to sleep with her anyway because it's me he really loves. He couldn't leave her before because their son was ill, but he's getting better now and—'

'How many children do they have?' asked Kate.

'Two,' Sara replied, 'two boys…' Her face crumpled. 'And now there's going to be another. She…she, his wife, she couldn't be in here for anything else, could she?' She was almost pleading with Kate now, willing her to say that sometimes patients came to the department for some other reason.

'No, Sara,' said Kate quietly. 'I'm sorry, but she couldn't be here for any other reason.'

'I have to phone him,' said Sara at last. 'There must be some explanation. Philip wouldn't have lied to me like that. She must have been having an affair as well! Yes, that's it.' Her eyes brightened. 'That must be it. She's been having an affair to punish him even more and she got pregnant by this other man. That baby isn't Philip's—I know it isn't. *This* one is Philip's!' She moved her hands over the smooth dome of her stomach, the gesture both proud and protective.

When Kate left Sara, the girl was already trying to contact Philip Browne at the company where they were both employed, while Nicole Browne, when Kate went into the labour suite, was awaiting the arrival of the same man.

'My husband is on his way in,' Nicole told Kate, when Kate tentatively enquired. 'His job takes him away from home quite a bit, but fortunately he's here at the moment, although he'd already left for work when my waters broke this morning.'

'How are your contractions, Nicole?' asked Kate.

'They were very strong at first, that's why I called for

an ambulance. I was told that third babies are sometimes apt to make speedy arrivals, but since I got here I have to say they seem to have eased up.'

'That's very often the case,' Kate replied. 'How about I take a look and see what's happening?'

'Well,' she said after examining Nicole, 'your cervix is six centimetres dilated so I would say those contractions will pick up again very soon, and the baby's heartbeat is strong.'

'It's a little girl,' said Nicole, her round face beaming. 'We already have two boys and when I found out I was having a girl I was over the moon. So was my husband— he dearly wants a daughter. You see, Sister—' she lowered her voice '—our marriage hit a rocky patch recently, but we've worked at it and this baby is going to set the seal, so to speak. Needless to say, my boys are thrilled—they can't wait to see their little sister.'

'We have one of those situations on our hands which unfortunately has become all too familiar on Maternity but which nevertheless requires careful and discreet handling.'

Kate glanced round her office at her assembled staff and suddenly realised that Tom had slipped into the room and was leaning against the closed door, his arms folded. It was unusual for him to attend a staff conference unless he was directly involved, and whereas in the past Kate would have thought little of it now, because of recent events, she found she was acutely aware of him. So much so that when she attempted to continue she found that her voice was suddenly husky. She cleared her throat and swallowed.

'Two days ago, as you will know,' she managed to continue at last, 'we admitted Sara Millington. She is thirty-eight weeks into her pregnancy and with raised blood pressure—her labour is to be induced today. She told us that her next of kin is her boyfriend, Philip Browne, and he has already visited her. Early this morning we admitted Nicole Browne. She was in fairly strong labour when she arrived and her membranes had ruptured. Since then, however, her contractions have subsided. As you will no doubt by now have worked out, Nicole Browne is Philip Browne's wife. I fear there may well be scenes before the day is out and I suggest you will need to be models of tact and discretion when dealing with these two ladies.'

'How do we know all this?' asked Natalie.

'Sara Millington recognised Nicole Browne when she arrived,' Kate replied. 'Fortunately her husband didn't bring her in,' she went on. 'She arrived by ambulance but it can only be a matter of time before Philip Browne arrives and will be forced to make a decision as to which woman he visits—Sara, whom he visited last night, or his wife Nicole. Or maybe he will visit them both.'

'Ye gods!' Natalie passed a hand across her brow in an exaggerated gesture. 'The messes people get themselves in!'

'Yes, quite,' Kate replied dryly, 'but as in every other situation that comes into Maternity, our job is to deliver healthy babies and give the best, most professional care to the mothers. It is not for us to judge, condemn or criticise any moral aspect of the situation.' She glanced round at the others once again, only too aware of Tom's eyes upon her. 'Is that clear?' she asked.

There were nods and murmurs of agreement, then Natalie spoke again, voicing the question that must have been uppermost in many minds. 'What about the wife?' she asked. 'Does she know about Sara?'

'She apparently knew of her husband's affair,' Kate replied, 'but believes it to be over. Likewise Sara believes that Philip Browne is about to leave his wife to be with her. But, irrespective of what either of these ladies do or do not know, we can assume there may well be trouble. I don't need to remind you that what you have been told is, of course, in the strictest confidence. But our job is to maintain the smooth running of this department and that is why I have decided to divulge these details to you.'

Moments later the staff had filed out of Kate's office and made their way back to their various tasks—all except Tom, who lingered.

'Mr Fielding?' asked Kate. 'Is there anything I can help you with?' She was aware of the brisk, matter-of-fact tone of her voice, something she had consciously decided to adopt in any dealings with Tom while at work, just as she was aware that Natalie had cast an interested backward glance at them both before leaving the office.

'Kate?' he said. 'Is there anything wrong?'

'No,' she said quickly, 'of course not.'

'It's just that you seem…different somehow this morning. Since the weekend really, if I'm honest, but somehow even more so today.'

'Different from what?' she asked as she began tidying a pile of folders on her desk.

'From how you usually are,' he said softly, 'and certainly from how you were on Saturday. I was beginning to wonder whether I had overstepped the mark in asking you out—or even if I'd upset you in any way.'

'No,' she said at last, allowing her gaze to meet his but uncomfortably aware that the two of them could still be seen through the glass panel on the door. 'No, of course you haven't, Tom.'

'Then why the brisk manner?'

'I'm sorry if I appear that way, but I really do think that we should keep our private and our professional lives totally separate.'

'Yes, I agree.' He nodded. 'To a point anyway, but not to the extent where I am reduced to a quivering wreck because I think I may have upset you.'

She laughed at that—the unlikely image of the cool, serious Tom Fielding reduced to a quivering wreck.

'That's better,' he said at the sound of her laughter. 'That's more like the Kate I've come to know.'

'I'm sorry, Tom,' she said, her guard down now, 'but I want to avoid gossip in the department because I don't think it makes for a good professional working environment. Already I fear vibes are being picked up.'

'Vibes?' He raised his eyebrows.

'Yes,' she replied, growing serious again. 'By Natalie. She is a friend of mine but she is also something of a matchmaker…' She trailed off, suddenly uncomfortable that he should misinterpret what she was saying, worried that he might think that in her mind their few meetings and him asking her out constituted more than it did. But she needn't have worried because his eyes crinkled at the corners and it was his turn to laugh.

'You think she has us walking down the aisle?' he asked, merriment dancing in his grey eyes.

'Well, perhaps not that exactly,' Kate replied, 'but she will, no doubt, seize on the fact that you have asked me out.'

'She doesn't know that?'

'No.' She shook her head. 'Neither does she know you came to lunch at the weekend, although heaven only knows how I've managed to avoid telling her. She knows about the bowling and our visit to your house—I'm afraid I had to tell her about those. She's a good friend, you see,' she added, compelled somehow to defend Natalie, 'and she's been a tremendous help to me since Liam died.'

'Hey,' he said softly, bending his head as he tried to look

into her eyes, and for some extraordinary reason causing her heart to miss a beat. 'You don't have to explain anything to me. OK, so Natalie is your friend. OK, so she knows about our meetings. It really doesn't matter to me. If I'm honest, gossip doesn't worry me either, but if you feel it would undermine the efficient running of the department then I'm happy that we keep things quiet. Just as long as you aren't having second thoughts about us seeing each other.'

'No,' she said, 'no, of course not.'

'In that case, I guess I'd better get back to the fray. I'll go and see Nicole Browne first, then Sara Millington. Maybe, under the circumstances,' he added with a wry grin, 'I'd better wear a hard hat.' As he spoke there came the sound of a knock and Mary put her head round the door.

'Sorry, Kate,' she said, 'but I thought I'd better tell you that Philip Browne has just arrived. I've asked him to wait in the relatives' room.'

'All right, Mary, thank you.' Kate nodded then gave a little sigh. 'I think it might be me in need of that hat,' she added ruefully. 'Well, best get it over with. I wonder which one he's come to see.'

'I'll come with you,' said Tom.

'You don't have to,' Kate replied quickly. 'I'm sure I can cope.'

'I don't doubt that,' Tom replied. 'I just thought you might like me aboard for this.'

Kate hesitated then, taking a deep breath, she said, 'Yes, all right, Tom, thanks—it probably would be better if we both saw him.' Together they left Kate's office and, with Kate deliberately avoiding Natalie's speculative gaze, made their way past the nurses' station to the relatives' room.

Philip was standing with his back to the door, gazing out of the window, and it was almost impossible to guess what his thoughts might be as he stood there, waiting for both his wife and his girlfriend to give birth. Kate had already seen him previously when he had visited Sara and he had struck her as a perfectly ordinary young man in his thirties—by no means the womaniser he was now being presented as.

He turned to face them and Kate noticed he was dressed in the dark suit and white shirt that he no doubt wore for his office job. His dark hair was cut very short and there was a wary expression in his eyes as his gaze flickered from Kate to Tom then back to Kate again.

'Mr Browne, I'm Sister Ryan,' said Kate. 'And this is Mr Fielding, who is our consultant obstetrician.'

'There's nothing wrong, is there?' Philip blinked several times.

'No, Mr Browne.' It was Tom who answered. 'There's nothing wrong. I'm about to examine your wife.'

'But she came in an ambulance…?'

'It was a precautionary measure,' Kate explained. 'Her waters had broken and she had started labour. I gather she couldn't contact you so she phoned for an ambulance. Since her arrival her contractions have eased somewhat, but we don't have any reason to believe there is a problem.' She paused and glanced at Tom then continued, 'The only thing we fear we may have a bit of a problem with is the fact that Sara Millington is also soon to give birth.'

'Does Nicole know that Sara is here?' asked Philip. He looked embarrassed and uncomfortable, and Kate noticed a thin line of beads of sweat on his upper lip.

'No, she doesn't,' said Kate, 'but unfortunately Sara knows that Nicole is here.'

'How does she know that?' There was another emotion in Philip's eyes now, whether shock or panic Kate wasn't sure.

'She saw her arrive,' Kate replied simply. 'As you know, the entire maternity department is very open-plan and although your wife was taken straight to the labour suite on her arrival, Sara saw her being wheeled past the antenatal bay.'

'So how is Sara—what did she say?' he asked. He was still wary, as if uncertain how much had been divulged.

'She seemed surprised to see your wife in Maternity,' said Kate bluntly, 'but none of that is our concern, Mr Browne. Our concern is totally for the welfare of our patients, in this case both your wife and Sara, and for the safe delivery of their babies.'

'Sara is already suffering from high blood pressure,' said Tom suddenly. Both Kate and Philip turned to him. 'We have planned to induce labour this morning so I wouldn't want any undue strain put on her. Maybe you could bear that in mind when you speak to her.'

'I can arrange it that your wife doesn't see Sara or even know that she is on the unit,' said Kate, 'but that has to be your decision. Is that what you would like?' she prompted when he appeared to hesitate.

'Yes,' he said at last, and Kate thought she saw something like relief in his eyes. 'Yes, please.'

'As far as I know, your wife shouldn't have any complications,' Kate went on. 'As this is her third delivery it should be quite straightforward. I imagine she will be discharged after a few hours, as she was with her last baby. I understand she wants you to be present at the birth.'

'Yes.' Philip ran one hand over his hair in a gesture that implied growing distraction. 'Yes, she does.'

'I'll go and examine her now,' said Tom.

'You stay here for the moment, Mr Browne,' Kate said as she turned towards the door, 'then I'll come back and let you know what's happening.'

'I wouldn't be in that man's shoes for anything,' said Tom darkly as he and Kate left the relatives' room.

'I couldn't imagine you getting yourself into that sort of situation in the first place,' said Kate.

'Maybe not.' He shrugged. 'But it's amazing how these situations escalate and spin out of control.'

In the labour suite, they found that Nicole's contractions had started again.

'I can't understand why my husband isn't here,' she muttered between contractions.

'He's on his way,' said Kate. 'Maybe he's been held up in traffic.'

When she returned to the relatives' room, alone this time as Tom had to go to Theatre to scrub up for a Caesarean section, she found Philip sitting with his head in his hands and for the first time she felt a stab of pity for him.

'I don't know what I'm going to say to Sara,' he said, looking up as Kate came into the room.

'I don't know how you are going to solve your problems, Philip,' she said, shutting the door behind her and sitting down beside him, 'but, like Mr Fielding said, the important thing at the moment is to keep calm and for us to get both babies safely delivered.'

'You must think I'm absolutely terrible,' he said, lifting both hands in a gesture of near despair, 'but, really, I never meant for any of this to happen.'

'It isn't for me to moralise. Neither, by keeping these two ladies apart, are we being party to any deception,' said Kate. 'Our main aim, as I said, is to deliver two healthy babies and to ensure the well-being of both mothers.'

As she finished Philip immediately began speaking, as if it was suddenly imperative to him that she should understand him and what had happened. 'I want to tell you about all this,' he said.

'You don't have to,' Kate replied quickly, 'and I do have a lot to do.'

'Please,' he said, and there was anguish in his eyes now.

'All right.' With a little sigh Kate sat down and prepared to listen.

'I work with Sara,' he said after a moment. 'I didn't plan to fall in love with her—it just happened. We used to take our lunch to the park each day and it was at a time when Nicole and I had been going through a rough patch in our marriage. I started seeing Sara outside the office and…I don't know…I suppose we became careless. Anyway, Nicole found out and there were some dreadful scenes. She told me I had to give Sara up or get out. My boys begged me to stay… It was a ghastly time.' Leaning forward in his chair, he linked his hands together.

'What did you do?' asked Kate.

'I gave Sara up,' he replied, 'or at least I tried to, and Nicole and I decided to try for another baby in an attempt to save our marriage, but after a while Sara and I slipped back into seeing each other again… It was so difficult not to, what with us working together.'

'And she also became pregnant,' said Kate.

He didn't answer immediately and then, as if reaching a decision, he admitted, 'She stopped taking the Pill without telling me.' When he saw Kate's expression he said, 'I'm not trying to make excuses. I love Sara, I really do, but I also love Nicole…and my boys.'

'You know, Philip,' said Kate gently, 'you are the only one who can sort this mess out.'

'I know.' His voice sounded choked now.

'I don't know how you are going to do it and I can't help you with it,' said Kate, 'but what I do know is that you can't do anything today. You owe it to both of them to let them have their babies in peace.'

'Yes. Right.' Taking a deep breath, he stood up. 'Where do I go first?'

'You must go to Nicole,' said Kate. 'She is expecting you to be by her side when she gives birth. You can see Sara later, if you wish.'

'Very well.' He nodded. 'Thanks, Sister,' he added.

'What for?' asked Kate.

'For listening,' he replied helplessly.

'Well, I think he's a rat,' said Natalie.

It was much later and Kate and some of the others were taking a well-earned break in the staffroom.

'That was my immediate reaction,' said Kate, 'but after talking to him I came to the conclusion that he had got himself in so deep that he simply didn't know how to get out of it.'

'Surely you're not taking his part?' Natalie turned to her in amazement.

'No, not really.' Kate shook her head. 'He shouldn't have allowed himself to stray in the first place then none of this would have happened.'

'I blame the girlfriend,' said Mary. 'Her type think nothing of breaking up a happy marriage.'

'It couldn't have been that happy if he was willing to look elsewhere,' observed Melissa as she poured herself a second cup of coffee. 'I would say the wife is as much to blame as anyone else.'

'Maybe they are all a bit to blame,' said Kate with a sigh, 'but, as we said before, it isn't for us to judge—all that we should be concerned with is that Nicole was delivered of a healthy baby girl and has been discharged, and that Sara is well into labour.'

'Do we know where Sara is going after she is discharged?' asked Melissa.

'She said to her mother,' Kate replied, 'which I think, under the circumstances, is just as well.'

'What do you think he's told Sara?' asked Natalie curiously.

'I don't know.' Kate shook her head. 'But Sara had assumed that Nicole must have been having an affair herself to get pregnant. Maybe Philip is letting her go on believing that, for the time being anyway.'

'Surely he won't be able to get away with two-timing both of them any longer?' said Mary Payne.

'No,' Kate replied. 'I think he's well aware the time has come that he has to finally make a decision and stick to it.'

'Do you think he really does love both of them?' asked Melissa, looking around at the others.

'Probably,' said Natalie with a shrug, 'but that's not the point. He's married to Nicole, she's his wife and his first loyalty has to be to her.'

'But he told Sara he was going to leave his wife,' protested Melissa.

'That's as may be,' said Mary, 'but in my experience men rarely leave their wives and when they do they very often return to them further down the line. I even know of a couple who divorced and the man remarried, only for him to go back to his ex-wife fifteen years later.'

Mary's words left Kate feeling vaguely uneasy, although she couldn't exactly say why that should be. Was it because she herself was on the brink of starting a relationship with a divorced man? But was she, she asked herself? Surely the friendship she had with Tom Fielding hardly constituted the type of relationship that need have her questioning whether or not he still loved his ex-wife?

She drained her coffee-mug and was about to rise to her feet when the intercom on the coffee-table suddenly bleeped. She leaned forward and flicked the switch, and

Rachel's voice came through, informing them that Sara was about to give birth.

'I'll go,' said Kate. 'Would someone please page Mr Fielding? He said he wanted to attend this one.'

When Kate entered the labour suite she found Rachel Paterson in attendance on Sara, and Philip seated beside her. She found herself wondering how on earth he'd managed to get his wife and baby daughter home and get back to the hospital without any questions being asked.

'She's fully dilated,' said Rachel, as Kate pulled on her surgical gloves and donned a large plastic apron to protect her uniform. 'And she's wanting to push, aren't you, Sara?'

Sara nodded then gasped as another contraction seized her and she clutched at Philip's hand.

Ten minutes later Tom arrived and, after examining Sara, decided that he would perform an episiotomy.

'What's that?' Philip looked alarmed.

'It's all right, Mr Browne,' said Tom reassuringly. 'It's simply a little cut performed under a local anaesthetic which will help the baby's passage into the world. If we didn't do it Sara would tear quite badly, she would be more uncomfortable and it might take longer to heal with a greater risk of infection.'

'Just let them do it, Philip,' said Sara weakly. Turning to Kate, she said, 'He does worry about me so, but maybe I shouldn't complain.'

Kate turned away, for once quite lost for words. Drawing up the injection of local anaesthetic, she handed the syringe to Tom who administered it and, after waiting a few moments for it to take effect, performed the episiotomy. The birth came after several more very strong contractions, and as Sara groaned and pushed for all she was worth Philip supported her neck and shoulders reassuring and encouraging her, for all the world like any devoted husband.

It was Tom who delivered the baby as it emerged into the world with one long drawn-out wail. 'You have a son, Sara,' he said as he lifted the baby onto Sara's chest. 'A fine, healthy boy.'

'Oh, Philip,' she cried, 'look, isn't he lovely? He looks just like you, with all that dark hair.'

In the excitement and emotion of the moment Philip admired his new son, and as he looked up and his gaze met Kate's she saw there were tears in his eyes. In that moment she knew his decision had just become all the more difficult.

He declined the offer to cut the cord and after Kate had performed that task she gathered up the baby and took him to the far side of the room where she cleaned him up and weighed him while Tom sutured Sara's cut.

'We've decided on a name,' said Sara, who had been lying quietly with Philip holding her hand.

'Oh, yes,' said Tom, 'and what is that?'

'Well, definitely Philip after his father,' Sara replied, 'and we thought Thomas after you.'

'I'm honoured,' said Tom. 'It's great to have such a handsome little fellow named after me.'

Kate wondered what Sara would have thought had she known just how many little boys born at Ellie's bore the name of the consultant obstetrician.

'We are going to take you over to the postnatal ward now,' said Kate, as Tom finished suturing.

'And the baby?' asked Sara anxiously.

'Of course,' Kate replied. 'He goes where you go.'

'Did you hear that, Philip?' said Sara. 'We are a proper family now.'

Just once, briefly, before Rachel took them to Postnatal, did Philip acknowledge Kate and Tom. 'Thank you,' he said, his gaze flickering from one to the other. 'Thanks for everything.'

They both knew he wasn't only referring to the safe delivery of his son but to the diplomatic way they had handled the events of the day.

'What do you think he will do?' asked Tom as the doors closed behind them.

'I think he'll stay with his wife,' said Kate. 'I think he had already decided to do that once he knew she was pregnant, but he couldn't bring himself to tell Sara, especially when he knew she also was expecting.'

'She's going to be very upset when she finds out,' said Tom.

'Yes,' agreed Kate, 'I fear she will.'

'It's been quite a day.' Tom peeled off his surgical gloves. 'Do you have time for a drink?'

'I'm sorry,' said Kate, 'I don't. I'm already late as it is, but I wanted to see Sara safely delivered. I should have been home hours ago.'

'Me, too,' he said with a grin. 'Never mind. Friday is still on, I hope?'

'Oh, yes,' she said, her gaze meeting his and her heart giving that delicious little lurch again at what she saw there. 'Of course it is.'

Later, as Kate drove home, she once again felt that pang of unease, brought on, no doubt, by the events of the day, but quickly she tried to dismiss the thoughts as once again she told herself her relationship with Tom bore absolutely no resemblance to the tortuous triangle Philip Browne had created for himself. Philip was married and his wife deserved to come first in his affections, whereas Tom was divorced and his love for his ex-wife was long over. So, if that was the case, why this sense of unease? She had no answer to that—she could only hope that in time it would go away.

CHAPTER SEVEN

'It's not fair! Why can't *we* go?' demanded Siobhan, her face flushed with indignation.

'I'm sorry,' said Kate, trying to keep her voice as steady as possible, not wanting confrontation with her daughter, particularly before going out for the evening, 'but it's all arranged now.'

'But why can't we all go?' Clearly Siobhan hadn't finished.

'Well, for a start, I expect Joe and Francesca are with their mother and that's probably why Mr Fielding has just asked me.'

'I think he's asked you because he wants to be your boyfriend,' said Connor solemnly, joining in the argument.

'Don't be stupid,' said Siobhan, rounding on her brother. 'Mum doesn't want a boyfriend. She had Daddy…' She trailed off in confusion, as realisation suddenly appeared to sink in. 'Mum…?' she said uncertainly.

Kate took a deep breath. 'I very much doubt that Mr Fielding wants to be my boyfriend,' she said. 'All that has happened is that he has asked me to go out for a meal with him.'

'Yes,' said Connor philosophically, 'just like you were his girlfriend.' With his quick grin he went out of the room, leaving Kate alone with Siobhan.

'Would it bother you if I did have a boyfriend?' Kate gently asked her daughter.

'I don't know.' Siobhan began kicking the edge of the

114

hearthrug with the toe of her trainers. 'What about Daddy?' Predictable tears filled her eyes at mention of her father.

'You know something, Siobhan,' said Kate after a moment's consideration. 'I used to worry about that—that if I went out with someone else it would in some way be disloyal to your father. But when I told Aunt Bessie that, do you know what she said?'

'No—what?' Siobhan rubbed at her eyes.

'That Daddy himself had once said to her that if anything happened to him he hoped I could find happiness with someone else.'

'Do you think that's what will happen—with Mr Fielding?' said Siobhan with a sniff.

'Darling, I have no idea, and really you mustn't read more into this than there is. I have known Mr Fielding for a long time and tonight is about two people, colleagues who have also become friends, sharing a meal together.'

'Will you sleep with him?' asked Siobhan.

'Siobhan! Of course not!' Kate stared at her daughter, perturbed that she should even think such a thing. 'Whatever gave you such an idea?'

'Dunno.' Siobhan shrugged. 'Except that Chloe said her cousin slept with her boyfriend and they'd only been out together once.'

'Well, I can assure you that isn't going to happen, and maybe Chloe's cousin should think about what she's doing. The next thing we know is that she'll be pregnant.'

'No, she won't,' said Siobhan. 'She said they used a condom.'

With Kate searching for a suitable reply, Siobhan stood on tiptoe in front of the large mirror that hung over the mantelpiece and screwed her hair up into a knot on the top of her head. 'Actually,' she said, studying her new appearance with apparent satisfaction, 'it could be rather neat if you and Mr Fielding got together. On the other hand, if you married him, what would that make Joe and me?'

'Stepbrother and -sister,' replied Kate. 'But—'

'And can stepbrothers and -sisters go out together...or get married?' Siobhan interrupted, tilting her head first to one side, pouting her lips as she did so, and then to the other.

'Yes, I think so,' Kate replied.

'Oh, well, that's all right, then,' Siobhan replied.

Not wanting to get any more involved in that particular conversation, Kate made her way to her bedroom and for a moment stared at the dress she'd hung on the wardrobe door. She'd bought it that afternoon on a sudden impulse on her way home, in a little dress shop in town. She'd agonised over what she should wear on her date with Tom, and while she had played the whole thing down to Siobhan, that it was simply a meal between colleagues and nothing more, she'd known in her heart that she wanted to make an effort with her appearance. But at the same time she'd been only too aware there was little in her wardrobe to fit the occasion.

She'd chosen the proverbial little black dress, knowing that it would take her anywhere and at the same time be an asset to her wardrobe for future occasions. It was made of a soft, silky material, hanging straight from slender shoulder straps and swirling gently at the knee, and when, after showering and carefully applying her make-up, Kate stepped into it and drew it up over her body, the sensuous feel of the material made her feel like a million dollars. And if she was still in any doubt about her appearance, it was laid to rest when she walked into the sitting room and Aunt Bessie and the children caught sight of her.

'That's a new dress!' exclaimed Siobhan.

'You look very nice, dear,' said Aunt Bessie with a little smile.

'Just like someone on the telly,' said Connor, which, coming from him, was praise indeed, for he hardly ever noticed what anyone was wearing.

'Well,' said Kate a little nervously, 'I thought I should make a bit of an effort.'

'I bet he'll want to be your boyfriend now,' said Connor with a grin.

'Don't be silly, Connor,' said Kate. 'Mr Fielding is still my boss. Oh,' she exclaimed as the doorbell rang, 'that'll be him now.'

'Have a good time, dear,' said Aunt Bessie, 'and don't worry about these two. I'll see they do their homework before bed.'

It was something of a relief in the end to leave the room, away from Aunt Bessie's knowing smile and her children's speculative glances. Honestly, she thought as she hurried down the stairs, they were nearly as bad as Natalie with her matchmaking, and had done nothing to allay her own nervousness for, if the truth were known, she was feeling just like a teenager on her first date.

Tom was waiting for her on the doorstep, while behind him in the lane stood the Mercedes convertible.

'Hi,' he said, his gaze briefly taking in her dress and her best cerise pink jacket, which she had draped around her shoulders. 'You look lovely.'

It was the first male compliment she had received for a very long time, so long, in fact, that she had almost forgotten how to receive one, and she found herself almost saying that this was just something she'd found in the wardrobe and flung on at the last moment. But just in time she remembered, smiled and inclined her head. 'Thank you,' she said.

He looked casually handsome in light-coloured chinos, a black cotton poloneck shirt and a soft, tailored leather jacket. 'I thought,' he said as he opened the car door for her, 'that we'd take a run down to the coast—there's a rather nice little restaurant I know that serves the most delicious seafood. What do you think?'

'Sounds wonderful,' she said. 'I adore seafood.' She leaned back in the luxurious leather seat, and as the car pulled away she glanced up at the house and was convinced she saw the sitting-room curtains twitch. They would all have been there, watching, she knew that—Siobhan especially, Connor and even Aunt Bessie, who wouldn't have been able to hide her curiosity.

Tom must have seen her smile for he threw her a sidelong glance. 'Did we have an audience?' he said.

'Undoubtedly.'

'Did you have any problems in getting away?' he asked as he eased the car out of the lane and onto the main road.

'Not really.' Kate shook her head and settled down into her seat, surprised to find that her nervousness had gone and she was looking forward to the evening ahead. 'Aunt Bessie was great, no problem at all with her looking after the children, and Connor—well, Connor is just Connor. He seems to take most things in his stride.'

'And Siobhan?' Tom raised one eyebrow.

'Ah, well, Siobhan is a little different.'

'She wasn't happy about us going out together?'

'Oh, I don't think she was too worried about that, although we did have to have a little talk about it not being disloyal to her father in any way.'

'She thought that?' Tom sounded concerned.

'It's new to her, that's all—me going out with another man—but, no, her main concern seemed to be the fact that she wasn't going, too. She seemed to think that it should only be family outings that we have.'

'Oh, dear,' said Tom with a laugh. 'I hope you told her that Joe and Francesca aren't coming with us.'

'Yes, I did.' It was on the tip of Kate's tongue to tell him what else Siobhan had said, about whether or not people should sleep together on the first date and about what relationship Joe would be to her if her mother and Tom were to marry, but she thought better of it, thinking that Tom might find the comments presumptuous. Instead, she said, 'What about your two? What do they think about us going out together?'

'Actually, I haven't told them yet,' he replied.

'Oh?' she said. 'Is there any reason for that?'

'Mainly because I haven't seen them,' he said.

Some slight inflection in his tone prompted Kate to say, 'But there is another reason, is that what you're saying?'

'Only that I have to tread very carefully in that respect, especially where Francesca is concerned. For a long time after her mother and I parted she cherished a dream that we would get back together again.'

'I believe that is the case with most children whose parents have parted,' said Kate.

'It happened once,' he said, and as she threw him a quick glance she noticed once again that pulse that throbbed at the edge of his jaw. 'After one of the monumental fights that Jennifer has with Max Oliver,' he went on, 'she packed their bags—hers and the children's—and came back.'

'That must have been upsetting for you.'

'It was. Not only for me—for us all, because I knew it wouldn't last.'

'Would you have been prepared to take her back?' she asked curiously.

Tom didn't answer immediately and she guessed he was

battling with some dark emotions which had probably until that moment never seen the light of day. 'I would have been prepared to try again for the sake of the children,' he said at last.

'So what happened?'

'She went back to him, as I knew she would, and things settled down again.'

'Surely now that she's married again, things are different?'

'Ah, but she isn't married,' he said quietly.

'Not married?' She frowned and threw him another glance.

'No, Max Oliver's wife wouldn't give him a divorce, so if they wish to marry they will need to wait the full five years.'

'You gave Jennifer a divorce,' she said.

'Yes.' He nodded. 'After two years. I didn't see any point in not doing so.'

They were silent after that, Tom apparently concentrating on the road ahead and Kate digesting the information he had just divulged, especially the fact that Francesca lived in hope that her parents would one day get back together again, and the fact that Jennifer and Max Oliver weren't married.

As they neared the coast, and somewhat to Kate's relief, Tom changed the subject and recounted a couple of anecdotes about fellow members of staff, together with such accurate and witty observations that Kate laughed aloud. She relaxed even more, realising there was much more to Tom than she had ever imagined.

He eventually brought the car to a halt in a little car park at the rear of a boatyard, and as Kate opened her door and stepped from the car the fresh salty air invaded her senses. To the accompaniment of the cries of the gulls, which swooped and wheeled overhead, they made their way through narrow, cobbled streets to the little restaurant, which was tucked away behind another building. They would surely have missed it if Tom hadn't known it was there.

They were shown to a table in a tiny bay window that overlooked the harbour and had a clear view of the sea beyond. 'The sunset should be pretty spectacular when it happens.' Tom glanced at his watch. 'Which should be in about an hour and a half.'

The food was delicious—from the salmon mousse and asparagus to the lobster accompanied by crisp white Chablis and the strawberry syllabub with shortbread that followed.

They talked endlessly—this time not of their previous lives and partners, or even of their children, but of themselves, their likes and their dislikes. They found to their surprise that they had a remarkable amount in common, from their taste in books, music and films—even food. They talked of travel, the places they'd visited, somewhat limited in Kate's case to family holidays in France and Spain, more adventurous in Tom's with visits to Thailand and India and skiing trips to Europe and Canada, and of the places they wanted to visit—Italy and Egypt for Kate, and Peru for Tom.

'Do you ski?' he asked her as they lingered over coffee.

'No.' She shook her head. 'Never had the opportunity.'

'In that case, I shall teach you,' he replied, his answer somehow setting the seal on the question as to whether or not their relationship had a future.

And when at last they left the restaurant after enjoying a truly spectacular sunset, watching until the very last sliver of orange had slipped into an indigo sea, it seemed the most natural thing in the world when Tom suggested a stroll along the sea wall. As they walked, he took her hand.

Only once did Kate think of Liam and of how it had been on her first dates with him—of the arguments with her father about her riding pillion on his motorbike, of the way he'd invariably dressed in jeans and leathers, and of how she'd been the envy of all her friends when she'd started to date the handsome Irishman with the powerful motorbike. All so very different from the man at her side now. Not that there was any question that he was any less handsome than Liam, she thought with a little smile, but he was different, very different. But, then, hadn't she too changed in those years since meeting Liam? So maybe…just maybe there was a chance…

'Penny for them,' he said suddenly, and she was jolted out of her daydream.

'For what?' she asked.

'Your thoughts,' he said. 'You were miles away.'

'I was just thinking how I can hardly believe this is happening,' she said, modifying her answer slightly, not wanting Tom to think even for a moment that she was comparing him to Liam in any way. 'That you and I are here like this.'

'I know,' he said, squeezing her hand as he spoke. 'It is pretty amazing, isn't it? I mean, we've known each other all this time, worked together, seen each other every day, and yet when it comes down to it we hardly knew each other at all.'

'I've been surprised to find just how much we have in common,' she said, 'but I would never have imagined that this would happen.'

'Why is that?' He raised one eyebrow. 'Because I wasn't your type, or, as Francesca would say, because you didn't fancy me?'

'No, of course not,' she said quickly, 'but—'

'Ah, so you *do* fancy me?' he said, cutting in swiftly.

'What I meant was,' she replied, skirting round his question, 'that we were poles apart. As far as we nurses are concerned, you consultants appear like a breed apart.'

'Oh, dear.' He pulled a face. 'You make us sound like some alien species.'

'Not at all,' she protested. When he laughed, she said, 'Just out of reach, that's all. But isn't the reverse also true?' she asked. By this time they had almost reached the end of the harbour wall.

'How do you mean?' He frowned.

'Well, would you consultants normally look amongst the nursing staff for serious relationships, or would you concentrate more on your fellow doctors?'

They stopped and in an involuntary movement turned to face each other.

'You'd be surprised,' he said with a grin, 'just what is said in the consultants' staffroom. I can assure you it isn't necessarily a case of not noticing—or fancying—the nursing staff, as much as a fear of being rebuffed. You have to remember, many consultants are over fifty and many nurses are in their early twenties.'

'So we are the exception to the rule?' she said lightly.

'I would say so, yes.' He looked down at her and from the light of an overhead harbour lamp she detected a gleam of amusement in his dark eyes. 'Shall we walk on the beach for a while?' he said suddenly, as if on impulse.

Kate only hesitated for a moment, considering the suitability of her high-heeled black sandals for such a pursuit. 'All right,' she replied. 'Why not?'

Still holding her hand, Tom led the way down the flight of stone steps that led to the beach. On the bottom step Kate stepped out of her shoes and slipped them into the beaded evening bag she was carrying. The soft, light-coloured sand still felt warm to the touch from the heat of the day's sun as they walked back to the jetty that formed one side of the harbour. The moon had risen and was casting a silvery pathway across the sea while high above them a handful of stars studded the darkening sky.

'I nearly asked you out before,' he said at last.

'Did you?' She threw him a startled glance.

'Yes, a couple of times,' he admitted.

'But you didn't?' she prompted, curious to know why.

'No, I didn't.' He paused. 'I wasn't sure you were ready,' he said. 'You seemed so vulnerable somehow, fragile even, after what had happened to you, that I held back…until…'

'Until that day at the bowling alley?' she said softly.

'Yes,' he agreed, 'until that day. Really, you know, Kate, I couldn't believe my luck that day. Oh, I know I could have asked you out at work but somehow it never seemed the right time. But meeting you there like that with your children, it seemed to me fate was giving me a little nudge and telling me there wouldn't be a better time.' As he spoke they stopped walking, and as before they turned once again to face each other, but this time Tom released her hand. Lifting his own hands, he took her face between them, tilting it upwards and gazing down into her eyes in the half-light.

Kate knew he was going to kiss her, but was she ready for this? Was it still too soon? There had been no one for her since the day she had met Liam and she still wasn't sure, was uncertain how she would react, afraid that she would be unable to respond to another man.

But at the touch of Tom's lips something magical began to take place, whether as the result of the moonlight, the wine or the chemistry between the two of them she had no idea, but as her lips parted beneath his and his fingers became entangled in her hair, she found herself not only responding to him but also becoming acutely aware of the awakening of some long-forgotten desire deep inside. With a little sigh she allowed her arms to go around him, drawing him closer, while he, with a small sound of surprised pleasure, released her face and put his own arms around her, gathering her against his body.

It had been a long time since Kate had known the strength of a man's arms around her, and with a sudden blinding flash she realised just how very much she had missed it—missed the warmth, the stirring of passion and the sharing of intimacy.

Her response to his kiss must have shaken Tom as much as it did her and when at last they drew apart they gazed at each other with a kind of wonder.

'Hey,' he said softly at last, 'you certainly are a lady of surprises.'

With his arm around her, they made their way slowly back along the beach to the jetty where they climbed the steps to the sea wall, and after Kate had slipped on her shoes once more they walked through the cobbled, moonlit streets to the car.

'Your place or mine for coffee?' asked Tom as he started the engine.

'Unless you want to share Horlicks with Aunt Bessie, it had better be yours,' said Kate lightly.

They both knew what the other meant, Tom in giving Kate an opportunity to refuse and she in agreeing to go back to his house with him. She couldn't quite believe she was doing so but at the same time she refused to look any further ahead than the present. Those incredible moments of shared intimacy on the beach had awakened something in Kate, something that had lain dormant for many long months, something she had imagined gone for ever, and she felt to a certain extent it was the same for Tom. By his own admission he had been deeply hurt by his wife's betrayal and unable to trust another woman. Could this now be a turning point for them both?

Her excitement and desire was almost at fever pitch by the time Tom drew into the drive of his home. He switched off the engine then stepped out onto the gravel drive before walking round to the passenger seat and helping her out of the car. The touch of his hand on her bare arm was like an electric shock and she felt a shiver of desire run the length of her spine.

He led the way into the house but they only got as far as the hallway before he turned to her with a groan and pulled her almost roughly into his arms again, his mouth seeking and finding hers, his tongue parting her lips. With a little sigh of satisfaction Kate gave herself up to the complete and utter thrill of being kissed by him again.

'I want you, Kate,' he murmured huskily between kisses. 'I've wanted you for a long time.'

'I want you, too,' she whispered. 'Maybe I shouldn't, but I do. I can't help it.'

Together they climbed the stairs and only once, after they had entered his bedroom and he had taken her in his arms again, did Tom appear to hesitate. 'Are you sure?' he said softly.

'Quite sure,' she replied.

He undressed her slowly, carefully removing each item of her clothing and draping them across a chair before leading her to the vast double bed with its cream and midnight blue covers. Swiftly he discarded his own clothing and all the while the tension and anticipation between them heightened with every glance and every touch. Just once did Kate know a moment's apprehension before he joined her on the bed, wondering if he would find her desirable. She need have had no such worries for as he lay beside her he said, 'You're beautiful, Kate.' And with a little sigh she relaxed and gave herself up to the delight of his love-making, which was exciting yet tender as, mindful of Kate's own needs, he held back, expertly and skilfully leading her to that secret place where all desires were satisfied and fulfilment was the prize.

Kate still couldn't quite believe that it had happened and as she lay in the large bed and stared up at the ceiling she found herself wondering what on earth she would say to her daughter. Turning her head, she looked towards Tom, only to find that he was watching her.

'Are you happy?' he asked with a lazy smile.

'Oh, yes,' she said, stretching luxuriously beneath the down-filled duvet. 'Very, very happy.'

'And no regrets?'

'No,' she sighed, 'no regrets.'

'I hadn't planned this,' he said almost apologetically. 'I want you to know that, Kate. I really didn't imagine this would happen when I asked you out for a meal.'

'I didn't expect it to happen either,' she admitted, 'but somehow it seemed—I don't know—almost inevitable really.'

'I felt that, too,' he agreed, adding after a short pause, 'I haven't felt like this for a very long time, Kate.'

'Me neither,' she said. 'And I wouldn't want you to think that I make a habit of this sort of thing.'

'What sort of thing?' With a grin he rolled over onto his stomach and, resting his elbow on the bed, cupped his chin in his hand and looked down at her.

'Sleeping with someone on the first date,' she replied.

'Oh, that,' he said. When her eyes widened at his apparent casualness, he chuckled and said, 'Well, if you're worried about that we can always call it our fourth date. That is, if you count those other times, even if the children were with us.'

'Talking of the children,' said Kate, 'do you know what Siobhan said to me when she knew we were going out tonight?'

'No, go on.'

'She asked me if we would sleep together.' Somehow it now seemed perfectly natural for her to tell him that.

'Well,' he said, 'I'm shocked.'

'Yes, so was I.'

'I mean,' he went on seriously, 'as if we would do such a thing! The very idea!'

Kate found herself laughing in spite of herself. 'What shocked me,' she said after a moment, 'was that she should even be thinking along those lines.'

'They grow up fast these days, Kate,' he said. Reaching out his free hand, he began twisting a strand of her hair. 'You know that by the age of some of the pregnant girls we see.'

'Yes, I know,' she said. 'I suppose it's just their casual approach to sex that worries me—their lack of commitment, if you like.'

'So what are you going to tell your daughter when she asks what we got up to tonight?' His eyes crinkled at the corners.

'Oh, Tom, I don't know... I really don't know.'

'Do you want some form of commitment?' he asked softly.

'I don't even know that,' she replied, looking up into his eyes, 'I haven't had time to think about it.'

'Well, I think perhaps you should,' he said lightly. 'And while you are thinking about it...' he let go of her hair and moved his hand under the duvet '…maybe this might help.'

'Oh, Tom…' She sighed deeply and arched her body to meet his.

'Mum, are you awake?'

'Hmm?' Kate turned over and looked at the bedside clock. It was nine o'clock.

'Oh, good.' Siobhan bounded into the bedroom and sat on the end of Kate's bed, 'You are awake. Francesca's just phoned, and guess what? She wants me to go over there this morning.'

'Over where?' Kate pushed her hair out of her eyes and struggled to sit up. It had been very late when Tom had brought her home and even later when, having lain awake and gone over and over in her mind every detail of that magical evening, she had finally fallen sleep.

'To her house,' said Siobhan impatiently. 'You know she has her own pony? Well, she said I can have a ride. Will you take me over there, Mum?'

'I don't know.' Kate frowned, trying desperately to clear her brain, wondering what Tom would think about her taking Siobhan to his ex-wife's home, wondering whether she even wanted to go.

'Oh, go on, Mum,' pleaded Siobhan, 'I can go, can't I? Please? I said I'd phone her back straight away. Oh, *please*, say I can.'

'Well, I suppose it will be all right,' said Kate doubtfully at last. 'Did she say what time?'

'Ten o'clock,' Siobhan replied airily.

Kate groaned. 'I guess that means I'd better get a move on,' she muttered as Siobhan leapt off the bed and headed for the door.

'What time did you get in last night?' Siobhan suddenly stopped in the doorway.

'It was pretty late,' said Kate warily. 'I'm not sure exactly what time it was.'

'So did you sleep with him?' asked Siobhan, arching one eyebrow. Before Kate could make any sort of reply, she held up her hands in a defensive gesture and said, 'Only joking. I know you wouldn't really do that—it's too gross.' With that parting shot she left the room, leaving Kate wondering whether her daughter thought it was gross that her mother should do such a thing on a first date, or whether she'd reached the conclusion that it was too gross to even think that her mother might want sex at all at her age. She had a suspicion the latter was the case.

Barely an hour later Kate drove up to the house where Francesca and Joe lived with Jennifer and Max. It was an old farmhouse, square, solid-looking and surrounded by a large paddock, fields and open farmland. Anyone could see them coming, Kate thought apprehensively as she approached the main building and brought the car to a halt alongside a white picket fence.

'Oh, look!' cried Siobhan, as a pony which had been grazing in the paddock lifted his head and cantered across to the fence, no doubt to investigate these newcomers and the possibility that they might have brought some interesting titbits. 'Oh, isn't he lovely? That must be Mr McGee—Francesca's pony.'

'There's another one over there.' Kate nodded towards a clump of trees on the far side of the paddock where a second horse grazed quietly in the shade.

'I think they all ride,' said Siobhan as they climbed out of the car. Even she seemed slightly overwhelmed by this evidence of their friends' lifestyle. Before they had a chance to walk up to the front entrance two dogs suddenly rounded the side of the house, one a black Labrador and the other a huge Rottweiler, both barking fiercely. Kate and Siobhan froze, their backs to the car.

'It's all right, they won't hurt you!' A woman appeared behind the dogs, a woman whom Kate recognised from the one brief time she had seen her, a woman with platinum blonde hair stylishly cut and dressed in jodhpurs and a hacking jacket. 'Jason! Oscar!' she commanded, 'Quiet!'

Immediately, to Kate's relief, the dogs fell silent and, after sniffing around herself and Siobhan and satisfying themselves that they didn't pose a threat, lumbered back to where they had come from.

'Sorry about that.' The woman tucked a strand of hair back behind one ear then held out her hand to Kate. 'Jennifer Fielding,' she said. Tom's surname on her lips came as a bit of a shock to Kate and she was glad that Tom had told her that his ex-wife and Max Oliver hadn't married. She barely touched Kate's hand.

'Kate Ryan,' said Kate. Turning to Siobhan she added, 'and this is my daughter, Siobhan.' She was saved from any awkwardness by the sudden appearance of Francesca in the doorway of the main house. She, too, was dressed in jodhpurs and carried a riding crop.

'Siobhan!' she exclaimed on catching sight of her friend. 'I guessed you had arrived when I heard the dogs! Hello, Mrs Ryan,' she added, smiling at Kate. For a fleeting moment Kate saw Tom in her smile and her heart turned over.

'Hello, Francesca,' she said. 'This is very good of you, letting Siobhan ride with you, but unfortunately she doesn't have any riding gear.'

'Mum!' muttered Siobhan in embarrassment. 'I've got jeans and trainers.'

'No, Siobhan,' said Jennifer Fielding briskly, 'your mother is quite right to be concerned. Francesca will fix you up with a hard hat, boots and some of her riding clothes—you look about the same size.'

'What time shall I pick her up?' asked Kate.

'I would have thought about four o'clock,' Jennifer replied.

Kate felt decidedly strange when a few moments later she drove away from the farmhouse, having declined Jennifer's offer of refreshment. Taking her daughter to ride with Francesca was one thing, but socialising with Tom's ex-wife was something else altogether and not something she felt she could cope with, especially after the night that she and Tom had just shared. She found herself wondering just how much Francesca or even Joe had told their mother about these new friends of their father's and themselves. No doubt she knew about the outing they had shared and the visits to each other's homes, but from the way Jennifer had eyed her up and down at the moment of their meeting Kate suspected that as a result of Siobhan and Francesca's constant phone calls to each other, Jennifer also knew that she and Tom had been out together the previous evening and that their relationship, which until then had simply been a family affair, had now entered a new, more intimate phase.

CHAPTER EIGHT

'YOU look like the cat that's got the cream,' murmured Natalie as Kate began to scrub up alongside her.

'I don't know what you mean,' protested Kate.

'Oh, yes, you do,' declared Natalie. 'You've been like it ever since you came in and I wouldn't think there would be any prizes for guessing why.'

'I'm sure I don't know what you're talking about,' replied Kate demurely, but a smile tugged at her mouth as she spoke.

'So it wouldn't have anything to do with a certain consultant and that every time he comes anywhere near you positively start to purr?'

'Natalie! Honestly!' Kate threw a quick glance over her shoulder to make sure they weren't being overheard but she still found herself smiling at the accuracy of her friend's observations.

'Well, it's true,' Natalie persisted. When Kate still declined to comment, she went on, 'So, are you going to tell me what's happened? Because it's pretty obvious that something has.'

'Maybe it has,' replied Kate, 'but here and now, when we are minutes away from an emergency Caesarean section, is neither the time nor the place.'

'Well, maybe not,' Natalie reluctantly conceded, 'but I'll see you later. How about a cappuccino in Angelo's after the shift?'

'OK,' said Kate with a sigh, 'you're on.'

Minutes later she was in Theatre and the patient, Maggie

Sumner, was wheeled in, accompanied by her husband Ted. This was Maggie's first baby and at forty-two she was considered an 'older mum', with all the risks that went with that dubious title. Kate knew that Maggie had suffered several miscarriages in the past, then, after a long period of time during which she hadn't conceived again, she and her husband had agreed to try IVF treatment. The second attempt had been successful but she had suffered problems throughout the pregnancy, ranging from high blood pressure and threat of miscarriage to swollen ankles, heartburn and painful bouts of sciatica. Now at thirty-eight weeks into the pregnancy, she had presented with a placenta praevia and Tom had decided to perform an emergency Caesarean section.

'What what does that mean?' Maggie, with tears in her eyes, had looked from Tom to Kate in anguish for her unborn child when the decision had been made.

'It means that the placenta wants to come before the baby,' Tom had explained.

'But will the baby be all right?' Maggie had implored.

'There is a slight risk, as with any operation,' Tom had replied, 'but there would be more risk if we didn't operate.'

'Do I have to have a general anaesthetic?'

'Not unless you want to. An epidural is perfectly adequate.'

'I want to be awake when my baby is born,' Maggie had said.

Now, an hour later, as Kate looked down at Maggie, who'd had her epidural, and Natalie prepared the screen, she smiled over her mask. 'Won't be long now, Maggie,' she said.

'Is Mr Fielding here?' asked Maggie.

'He's on his way.'

'It will be him, won't it?' asked Ted Sumner anxiously.

'We want it to be him, don't we, love?' Looking down at his wife over the top of his surgical mask, he took hold of her hand.

'Oh, yes,' said Maggie with a little sigh, 'we want it to be him. He's been so good to me throughout the pregnancy—he's a wonderful man.'

'He certainly is,' said Natalie cheerfully, her gaze meeting Kate's over the tops of their masks. 'Isn't that right, Sister?'

Kate was saved from having to reply to that particular question by the arrival of Tom himself, strolling into Theatre with no hint of the urgency that surrounded the case. Matt Forrester, whose presence was required to examine the baby as soon as it was born, accompanied him.

Kate found herself avoiding Tom's gaze, all too mindful of Natalie's earlier comments. It was true she had been incredibly aware of Tom that morning, but in view of what had happened between them at the weekend it was hardly surprising. In fact, if she was honest, she hadn't been able to wait to see him again, had found her heart thumping when she knew he was due in the department, and then, when she did first catch sight of him, she'd had to get a firm grip on herself as her heart had seemed to perform a series of gymnastics.

It would have to stop, Kate told herself firmly, at least while they were both at work. There was no way they could let what was happening in their private lives reflect on their professional relationship, especially now that Natalie had noticed. In future, she reminded herself almost fiercely, the two aspects would have to be kept distinctly separate.

'All ready, Maggie?' Tom looked down at his patient who smiled tremulously up at him and nodded.

'Shall we have some music in here?' Tom glanced at Ted Sumner. 'What would you like your baby to be born to—Bach? Mozart? Or maybe some jazz?' he asked hopefully, while Kate smothered a smile, knowing how keen Tom was on jazz. A throwback from his student days, he'd told her.

'Actually,' said Ted almost apologetically, 'we're into country and western.'

'Then country and western it shall be,' said Tom. 'I'm sure Sister can arrange that. Sister?' He turned to Kate and she was forced to meet his gaze. There was amusement there in those dark eyes, amusement and something else—something that sent a shiver of delight down Kate's spine.

Then that brief, light-hearted interlude was over and professionalism took over once more as Tom made the required incision. A little later, to the accompaniment of the Nashville sound, Maggie's and Ted's baby was lifted out into the world.

'It's a boy,' announced Tom, looking up over the screen at Maggie and Ted. 'Congratulations, you have a fine son,' he added.

'Is he all right?' asked Maggie anxiously.

'Here,' Tom replied, 'see for yourself.' After Kate had cut the cord he lifted the baby over the screen and placed him on Maggie's chest.

While Maggie and Ted spent precious moments becoming acquainted with their son and Tom cleared Maggie's uterus and began suturing, Matt stepped forward.

'I'd like to take a look at this little chap if I may,' he said. As Maggie reluctantly handed over her son, he held him gently in both hands. 'Does he have a name yet?' he asked.

'Yes,' said Maggie, glancing up at her husband. 'Stuart Edward.' Her voice sounded suddenly weak and very weary, and Kate leaned forward at the same time as the anaesthetist to check the readings on the pulse and blood-pressure monitors.

'Fine names,' observed Tom as Matt bore the baby to the far side of the room in order to carry out his examination. 'Right,' he added, 'we're just about all done here. I'm sure Maggie will be glad of a cup of tea now...'

'Blood pressure is dropping,' announced the anaesthetist suddenly.

There was a flurry of activity around the table as the green screen was removed then Maggie appeared to struggle for breath and the bleeping from the heart monitor gave way to a single ominous note.

'She's arrested!' said Kate.

'Get the crash trolley!' ordered Tom. 'Adrenaline, please. Sister. Start heart massage.'

While Tom administered the adrenaline injection Kate began the resuscitation routine while Natalie wheeled forward the crash trolley and defibrillator.

'What's happening?' A horrified Ted struggled to his feet and stared down at the still form of his wife. On the far side of the theatre Matt placed the baby into a waiting incubator and, together with a nurse, left immediately for the special care unit.

As Natalie moved Ted away from the bed while trying to reassure him, Tom took the pads from the defibrillator and approached Maggie. 'Stand clear!' he commanded, and when Kate ceased heart massage and stood back from the bed he applied the pads to Maggie's chest and administered a shock.

For a few seconds following the shock all eyes in the theatre turned to the heart monitor, which continued its single monotonous tone.

'There's no output,' said Kate.

'Again,' said Tom. 'Stand clear!' As everyone stood

back, he shocked Maggie for a second time and once again all eyes stared at the monitor. This time the indicator appeared to flutter, then a bleep was heard.

'We have an output,' said Kate, and a ripple of intense relief ran through the staff.

'Is she all right?' Ted was across the theatre and back at his wife's side before anyone could stop him.

'Her heart stopped for a moment there, Ted,' replied Tom.

'But why would that have happened?' Ted stared down at his wife, his anxiety plain for everyone to see.

'It could have been for any number of reasons,' Tom replied. 'We will need to do some tests to find out why. What we will do now is ask Sister to arrange for Maggie to be taken to our cardiac unit so these tests can be carried out.'

'What about the baby?' asked Ted frantically.

'Dr Forrester has already taken him down to the special care baby unit,' explained Kate gently. 'He'll be in the best hands possible there, Ted,' she went on, 'and you will be able to visit him shortly.'

During the following half-hour Kate arranged for Maggie to be admitted to the cardiac unit, and when the porters arrived to transport her she urged Ted to go with his wife. When they had left the theatre Tom peeled off his gloves and threw them into a waste bin. 'I can do without incidents like that,' he said.

'It wasn't your fault,' said Kate.

'Maybe not, but it was too close for comfort,' he replied tersely. 'I'm not in the habit of losing my patients, Sister, whether babies or their mothers. I want those test results as soon as they are available.' With that he strode out of the theatre, tearing off his theatre greens as he went.

'It couldn't have been his fault, could it?' asked Melissa,

wide-eyed at the drama. It was her first time in Theatre to witness a Caesarean section and Kate found herself wishing the occasion hadn't been so traumatic.

'It's highly unlikely,' Kate replied. 'If Mrs Sumner had had a known heart condition it would have been in her records and Mr Fielding would have treated her accordingly. As it was, there was no mention of anything untoward so what happened was probably unpreventable. Nevertheless, Mr Fielding will want to see the test results, if only to prove to himself that there wasn't anything he could have done.'

'Thank goodness he was able to resuscitate her,' said Melissa.

'Yes.' Kate nodded. 'Thank goodness indeed.'

'I wonder why Matt whisked the baby away so quickly,' mused Natalie.

'I don't know.' Kate shook her head. 'Let's hope it was just because of what was happening to Maggie and not because there was anything wrong with him.'

'I thought he looked very small,' observed Natalie.

'And he didn't cry, did he?' Melissa looked from Kate to Natalie as if seeking reassurance, then back to Kate.

'Let's not go jumping to any conclusions,' said Kate.

'No,' agreed Natalie, 'but I really hope all will be well with Maggie and the baby. They have waited so long for this to happen it would be too cruel for it to go wrong now.'

'Talking of small babies,' said Melissa as they set about cleaning the theatre, 'do we know anything about that baby who had breathing problems? You know, Dee Perren's little boy, the one who was born in the ambulance?'

'When I spoke to Sister Forrester last week she said he was a little fighter and was holding his own,' Kate replied.

'Now, if I can leave you two to finish clearing up here, I must get back to the ward.'

She found Tom at the nurses' station, seated before a computer and apparently trawling through Maggie Sumner's records. 'There's nothing,' he said, 'no mention of any cardiac problem either now or in the past.'

'I didn't for one moment imagine there would be,' said Kate soothingly. 'You wouldn't have missed something like that.'

'I'll still be glad when we get those results,' he said with a sigh. 'Let me know when they are through, will you, Kate?' He looked up at her and her heart went out to him at his obvious distress at coming so close to losing a patient.

'Of course I will,' she said, 'but they will take some time. They will want to do both an ECG and an echo-cardiogram and we have to remember that Maggie herself is recovering from surgery.'

'Yes, I know.' He clicked the mouse to close Maggie's file then with a sigh pushed his chair back from the desk.

'I dare say you could use a coffee?' she said softly.

'Are you offering, Sister Ryan?' The ghost of a smile crossed his face.

'Yes, Mr Fielding, I am,' Kate replied. He stood up and she led the way to her office and its ever bubbling pot of coffee. 'Now,' she said softly, 'sit down, Tom, and relax for a few minutes.'

'I wouldn't want too many mornings like that,' he admitted as Kate handed him a steaming mug of coffee and he added milk and sugar.

'No,' Kate agreed, 'but fortunately they are very rare. I think I can only remember that happening once before after a Caesarean section and on that occasion we couldn't save the patient.'

They sat in silence for a while, each busy with their own thoughts, then Tom looked up. 'Kate,' he said, 'I was on duty yesterday but when I got home I had a call from Francesca. She told me that you've met Jennifer.'

'Yes.' Kate nodded. 'I took Siobhan over to spend the day with Francesca—she had a lovely time,' she added.

'Yes, Francesca said they enjoyed themselves,' Tom agreed, 'but I did find myself wondering whether Jennifer knew we had been out together.'

'I don't know.' Kate frowned. 'Although I imagine that Siobhan would have told Francesca, in view of her comments to me on the subject. Whether Francesca told her mother or not I don't know, although…I have to say I rather got the impression she did know.'

'Yes, I would imagine that she did,' said Tom. 'Just as I would lay odds that Jennifer made sure she was around when you arrived. I would even go so far as to say that it was probably her and not Francesca who instigated the whole thing.'

'Does that matter?' Kate threw him a glance and was perturbed to see that he looked troubled. 'She was perfectly OK—not overly friendly but I wouldn't exactly have expected that. But civil enough.'

'No,' he said, setting his mug down on the desk and sitting back in his chair, 'it doesn't matter, of course it doesn't. You two would have had to have met each other sooner or later anyway, but years of experience have taught me to be wary of Jennifer's motives. Don't take any notice,' he said, standing up. 'It's probably just me being paranoid. Now…' He looked down at her and his tone and his expression softened. 'When am I going to be able to see you again?'

'I don't know, Tom,' she said, looking up into his eyes

and feeling her insides begin to melt at what she saw there. 'Did you have anything in mind?'

'Well, Joe and Francesca will be with me at the weekend so maybe we'd better do something with all the children then.'

'Sounds good,' she replied.

'But I can't wait that long—I need to see you on our own before that,' he said huskily, and at his words, deep inside Kate felt a sharp stab of desire. 'Would you be free on Wednesday evening and would Aunt Bessie oblige again?'

'I'm sure she would,' Kate replied. 'Siobhan won't like it but maybe the thought of a weekend treat might help.'

'Till Wednesday, then,' he said. He reached out and gently touched her cheek, his expression one of tenderness and wonder, as if he couldn't quite believe what was happening between them.

'Careful.' Kate's gaze flew to the door's glass panel but fortunately no one else was around. 'I think we may already be cause for speculation.'

'Let them,' said Tom. 'It doesn't worry me and, let's face it, it'll be a nine-day wonder then it will be someone else's turn.'

Angelo's Italian restaurant was just off Franchester High Street, close to the river, and with its green and gold striped awnings and tables and chairs set out on the wide pavement it had long been popular as a meeting place for staff from Ellie's. It was rumoured that Angelo and Maria Fabiano, quite apart from serving up the most delicious food imaginable, knew every member of the hospital staff by name.

It was Maria who greeted Kate and Natalie and showed them to a table in a far corner of the restaurant. 'I not seen you for a while,' she admonished, 'where you been?'

'Busy,' said Natalie, 'always busy, Maria. Barrie and me have been decorating our spare room and the kids have been involved in all sorts of things. And Kate…' She threw her friend a wicked glance. 'Well, Kate also has been up to all sorts of things since we were in here last. Isn't that right, Kate?'

'I've been busy, yes,' said Kate guardedly. Under Maria's close scrutiny she felt the colour touch her cheeks and hated herself for it. She was supposed to be a mature widow, for heaven's sake, and here she was, blushing like a fourteen-year-old.

'It'll be a man,' said Maria knowingly.

'How did you guess?' Natalie gave a peal of laughter.

'I know.' Maria held up her hands, 'I just know these things. Cappuccino?'

'Yes,' Natalie began, then, throwing Kate a quick glance, she added, 'On second thoughts, after the day we've just had, a glass of wine might be more appropriate, don't you think, Kate?'

'Yes,' Kate agreed, 'you could be right.'

'OK, two glasses of your best red, please, Maria, and a couple of your ciabatta melts.'

Maria bustled off to the kitchen and, on being given the order, Angelo looked out and waved to Kate and Natalie.

'Right,' said Natalie, settling back into her chair, 'come on, tell all. And don't tell me there isn't anything to tell because I won't believe you. I only have to look at your face to see that something has happened—and something good, if I'm not too much mistaken.'

Kate smiled and took a deep breath. She knew there was absolutely no point in not telling her friend the truth. 'Yes,' she said, 'you're right. Tom and I are seeing each other.'

'I knew it!' Natalie threw her head back in triumph. 'Well, Kate, all I can say is it's not before time and I'm absolutely delighted. It's time you had some love and excitement in your life again.'

'Hey, steady on,' said Kate, pulling a face but at the same time finding it difficult to hide her feelings. 'We've only been out on our own once.'

'When was it, where did you go? Come on, I want all the gory details...' Natalie trailed off as Maria came back to the table with their glasses of wine.

'I just get your melts,' she said, placing the glasses on the table, casting a speculative eye at Kate then hurrying back to the kitchen.

'It was Friday evening,' said Kate slowly. 'He picked me up from home and we went down to the coast.'

'Did you go in that four-wheel-drive of his or in that snazzy Mercedes?'

'Oh, the Mercedes,' Kate replied.

'Good. Then what?' Natalie leaned forward expectantly then had to sit back again as Maria brought their food, made sure they had everything they wanted then bustled off to greet more customers who had just arrived. 'Go on,' she said, taking a mouthful of wine and shaking out her napkin.

'Where was I?' asked Kate.

'On the way to the coast in Tom Fielding's Mercedes.'

'Oh, yes. Well, he'd booked a table at a little seafood restaurant overlooking the harbour. It was...well, it was magic really.'

'What did you have?' Natalie had clearly meant it when she said she wanted all the details.

'I had salmon mousse then lobster.'

'Did you get on well? Did you talk much?'

'Oh, yes,' said Kate. 'We talked about everything. I was amazed actually by just how much we have in common. We like the same books and films...'

'So what happened afterwards?' Natalie bit into her melt.

'We went for a walk,' Kate replied, 'along the sea wall and then back along the beach.'

'The beach?' Natalie frowned. 'I don't like walking on the beach. All that soft sand—it gets in everywhere.'

'I took my shoes off,' said Kate, her eyes misting slightly at the memory. 'And actually it was rather romantic,' she added defensively, then wished she hadn't as Natalie seized upon it.

'In what way romantic?' she demanded.

'Well, the moon was shining across the sea...'

'And?'

'And what?'

'Don't tell me that was all.' Natalie stared at her in exasperation.

'No,' Kate admitted slowly, 'no, of course it wasn't all, but really, Nat, I'm not sure I want to talk about—'

'Did you go on anywhere?'

'Back to Tom's place,' Kate admitted.

'Oh, right. Now we're getting somewhere.' Natalie gave a sigh of satisfaction.

'We could hardly go back to Copse End, not with Siobhan and Connor and Aunt Bessie there, could we?'

'Depends what you wanted to do,' said Natalie with a wicked gleam in her eye. 'OK for drinking coffee, I suppose, but anything else, well, I guess that would have cramped your style somewhat.' When Kate remained silent she cocked her head. 'It's all right,' she said, and her voice had lost its bantering tone. 'I don't want to hear any more—not unless you want to tell me, that is,' she added half-hopefully. After a quick glance at Kate's expression, in resigned fashion she added, 'All right, perhaps not.'

'Oh, Nat,' said Kate, 'it's not that I don't want to tell you anything...'

'No?'

'It's just that I'm afraid to say too much. It's very early days yet and I feel I may be tempting fate somehow. You see, I'm so happy at the moment. It's been such a long time since…well, since Liam, and if I'm honest there's a part of me that can't quite believe it…that feels it won't last.'

'But why shouldn't it last?' Natalie frowned.

'I don't know.' Kate shook her head. 'It's just so good and I suppose that I'm afraid that anything that good simply can't last.'

'Are you in love with him, Kate?' Natalie's voice was serious now with none of the teasing tone of earlier.

'I think I must be,' Kate replied at last, 'if being in love means your heart turning over whenever you catch sight of someone, if it means counting the minutes to when you can be together again, never mind the hours or the days, and if it means thinking of that someone every moment you are apart.'

'That's love,' said Natalie flatly.

They were silent for a while, Natalie apparently enjoying her ciabatta and Kate staring at hers and reflecting on what Natalie had just said. She had suspected she was falling headlong in love with Tom, but hearing Natalie confirm her symptoms was another thing altogether. Everything she had told Natalie was true—she did count the minutes until she could see him again, and since those few short hours when they had made love at his house Tom had been there in every waking thought. At night, he had dominated her dreams.

'Is there a reason for your caution?' asked Natalie at last, breaking the silence between them.

'Oh, Nat, I don't know.' Kate had been toying with her food, chasing it round her plate with a fork. Now she abandoned it completely and looked up. 'I just have this awful feeling sometimes that it can't last.'

'Well, now, let's think about this and see if we can't get rid of these fears,' said Natalie philosophically. 'He's free, isn't he?'

'Yes…' The pause was only minimal. 'He's divorced.'

'So that's not a problem, it's legal. What about the kids?'

'They seem more than happy with the situation.' Kate reflected. 'At least, Siobhan was rather protective of Liam's memory which, I suppose, is quite understandable, but even she seems to have got over that now. I also think she may have a bit of a crush on Joe.'

'Tom's son?'

'Yes.' Kate nodded. 'He's a really nice lad and I can quite see why Siobhan is smitten, although on the other hand she's far too young.'

'Too young?' Natalie stopped chewing and stared at her then gave a snort of derision. 'Oh, come on, Kate, you've got a short memory. What about when we were at school and we both had a crush on that boy in the sixth form— what was his name?'

'Gavin Coombes?' said Kate.

'Yes, that was him!' Natalie gave a hoot, which attracted the attention of other diners. 'Gavin Coombes! We were absolutely besotted by him. You had his initials carved all over your pencil case and I wrote his name all the way up my arm in indelible ink and it wouldn't come off and I got a detention. We couldn't have been any older than Siobhan is now.'

'No, maybe not.' Kate sighed then smiled as the memories of those far-off days flooded back. 'It's just,' she went on after a moment, 'that they seem so knowing these days about sex and contraception, but underneath they are still children.' She paused and threw Natalie a glance. 'You just wait until your Sophie is that age, you'll know what I mean then.'

'Don't.' Natalie gave a little shudder. 'Barrie says his greatest fear is that one day he'll see Sophie spread across the centre pages of some glossy men's magazine.' She paused then said, 'So that's Siobhan, who's happy with the situation, and presumably Joe, unless, of course, like many males, he's oblivious to all this adoration.'

'No, I get the impression he knows,' said Kate dryly.

'Like you say,' Natalie sniffed, 'more knowing these days. I doubt Gavin Coombes ever knew about us, and if he did he wouldn't have known what to do about it.'

'And if he had we would probably have run a mile,' Kate observed. 'I can't see Siobhan running a mile.' She gave a sigh.

'What about Connor?'

'Well, you know Connor. He's so laid back that he takes most things in his stride. Provided he has his computer and he gets to go swimming, he seems happy.'

'What about with Tom?'

'He responded well to him. In fact, the day we went to Tom's house and played in the pool Connor was in his element.'

'Family life.' Natalie nodded. 'It's what he misses now—having a man around.'

'I know…'

'And what about Tom's daughter—Francesca, isn't it?' Natalie rattled on, not giving Kate a chance to say more on the subject of Connor needing a father figure. 'Where does she fit into the equation?'

'Ah, Francesca—that's another story,' said Kate slowly.

'Oh,' said Natalie, raising her eyebrows, 'and why is that? Doesn't she like any of you?'

'It isn't that. I'm sure she likes us.' She paused then

frowned. 'At least, I hope she does. She and Siobhan seem
to get on very well—take Saturday, for instance. She invited Siobhan over for a day's riding—they have their own
horses. I took her over and…and Francesca's mother was
there…'

'You met her?' Natalie threw her a shrewd glance. 'How
was she towards you?'

'OK, I guess. Not exactly friendly, but I wouldn't expect
that. She must know we've all been spending time together
even if she doesn't actually know about Tom and me—
although I wonder about that.'

'So what's the problem?'

'I'm not sure really.' Kate shook her head. 'I think it was
just something that Tom said.'

'Are you going to tell me what this something was?'
asked Natalie when she fell silent.

Kate took a deep breath. 'It's probably nothing really,
but apparently Francesca lives in hope that Tom and her
mother will get back together again.'

'But don't you think all children from broken homes
hope for that?' asked Natalie, echoing the sentiments that
Kate herself had voiced to Tom.

'Yes, I guess…'

'So it isn't that that's bothering you…?'

'No, not exactly…'

'Then what?' she probed, and when Kate remained silent
she said, 'You're not afraid that Tom is still in love with
her, are you?'

'No,' Kate said quickly, too quickly. 'No, of course
not…' she added, but she knew she didn't sound too con-
vincing. Was it that she was worrying about?

'Has he given you any reason to suspect that?' Natalie
gave her no time to explore those particular possibilities.

Doubtfully Kate shook her head. 'No, not really, only

that he said that she and the man she lives with have never married…and that she came back to him once—Tom, that is—and he felt he should try to make their marriage work for the sake of the children.'

'And you're thinking he might have just said that when his real reason was that he was still in love with her?'

'Maybe.' Kate shrugged.

'She left him, didn't she? In the first place, I mean?'

'Yes, so she could be with this Max Oliver. Tom says she should never have married him, that she was always in love with this other guy. The reason she and Max haven't married is because his wife won't give him a divorce.'

'Hmm,' said Natalie. 'So what happened when she came back to Tom?'

'It didn't work out and she went back to Max.'

'Very unsettling for the children,' Natalie observed.

'And for Tom,' said Kate.

'Yes, and for Tom,' Natalie agreed. Narrowing her eyes, she looked at Kate. 'Know what I think?' she said.

'No,' said Kate, 'but I have the feeling you are going to tell me. In fact, I'd be glad if you did.'

'I think that you should just take things as they come. Don't try to force any issues, just enjoy what's happening. And who knows? In the end you may just find that everything will turn out for the best.'

'You think so?' asked Kate hopefully.

'Yes, I do,' said Natalie firmly. Draining her glass, she added, 'And even if it doesn't, you will have had a wonderful time with a really fantastic man, won't you?'

'Yes…'

'That is, always supposing that he is that fantastic?' She raised her eyebrows. 'Kate…?'

'Oh, yes,' said Kate with a sigh, 'there really isn't any doubt about that.'

'Well, there you are, then.' Natalie stood up and looked down at Kate. 'So, for heaven's sake, stop worrying about something that might never happen and just enjoy.'

CHAPTER NINE

'DO YOU have children, Sister Ryan?'

Kate looked down at the young woman in the postnatal bed who was attempting to feed her baby. 'Yes, Paula,' she said, 'I do. I have a girl and a boy.'

'So you know all about breastfeeding.' The woman pulled a face.

'It was a long time ago but, yes, I do remember thinking I would never get the hang of it, or rather my daughter wouldn't get the hang of it. But she did in the end, and it was well worth the experience. But just look at baby Jessica now—she's well away. I don't know what you are worrying about.' Reaching out her hand, Kate gently stroked the soft down on the baby's head, then with a smile she moved on to the next bed where another new mother, Vicki Perceval, was resting quietly, her baby son asleep beside her in a cot. Kate liked to visit the postnatal ward at least twice a day to check on the new mums and their babies. With its restful décor and pretty print curtains the atmosphere was different from that in Antenatal, not fraught with apprehension. Neither did it have the clinical efficiency of the labour suites. Here amongst the flowers and cards of congratulation was a sense of relief, even though at times the happiness was laced with emotion and anxiety as for the new mothers the realisation of responsibility sank in.

'How are you this morning, Vicki?' Kate asked.

'Much better, thank you, Sister.'

'And the bleeding?'

'It's eased up since last night.'

'And your temperature is down. Keep on like that and we could look at you and baby Bradley going home, perhaps tomorrow morning or, if Mr Fielding says so, even later today.' Bending over the cot, Kate gently lifted back the cellular blanket and looked down at the baby, who slept peacefully beside his mother.

'That's great.' Vickie smiled and picked up the paperback she had been reading. Then as Kate was about to move on she called her back. 'Oh, Sister,' she said, 'I hope you don't mind me asking, but is Mr Fielding your husband?'

'My husband?' Kate stared at her. 'No, of course not— my name is Ryan.'

'Yes, I know,' Vicki said, 'but some professional people keep their maiden names when they marry, don't they?'

'Yes,' Kate replied, 'they do. But I didn't. My husband's name was Ryan.'

'You're divorced?'

'No, I'm a widow,' Kate replied, and somehow, for the first time, as she said it, she didn't suffer that dreadful sinking feeling that she had always done in the past whenever she had told anyone.

'Oh, I'm sorry.' Vicki was clearly embarrassed. 'I didn't know.'

'Whatever gave you the idea that Mr Fielding was my husband?' Suddenly Kate was curious.

'I don't know…really, it was nothing.'

'No, go on, please, I'd like to know,' she said.

Vicky flushed and glanced round the ward as she spoke. 'It's just that you seem so in tune with each other somehow—we've all thought so, haven't we, girls?' She appealed to the three other occupants to back her up.

The women all nodded and one said, 'Yes, it's the way

he looks at you—as if you are the only woman in the world. It makes me feel all funny inside whenever I see it—I wish my husband looked at me like that. He did once but that was a long time ago.'

'I don't think mine ever did,' said another, and there was a ripple of laughter that dissolved any awkwardness.

'So we were wrong, then?' said Paula. When Kate didn't answer, continuing her perusal of some notes, she prompted, 'Sister?'

'Well, you were and you weren't,' said Kate, coming to a decision which she hoped she wouldn't live to regret. 'We aren't married, but we are seeing each other.'

'I knew it!' The woman who had complained about her husband never looking at her in that certain way punched the air in triumph in a gesture that reminded Kate of Siobhan.

Paula suddenly said, 'Talk of the devil…or in this case, maybe not…'

All eyes, including Kate's, flew to the entrance where Tom had suddenly appeared. He looked as handsome as ever with his white coat undone over his dark suit and a stethoscope draped around his neck. He stopped and looked around at the bright, expectant faces, then at Kate, his eyes narrowing slightly.

'You look a happy little band this morning,' he said uncertainly.

'Oh, yes,' said Vicki, 'we are, Mr Fielding, we are.'

Suddenly Kate couldn't cope with the situation any more and with a muttered apology she left Tom to the tender mercies of his patients. Once at the nurses' station she sent Natalie back to the postnatal ward to conduct the round with Tom, then she fled to the comparative sanctuary of her office, away from the knowing glances and speculative stares.

So even the patients were noticing now, she thought as she poured herself a badly needed cup of coffee and settled down behind a mountain of paperwork. The staff had sussed it ages ago, she knew that, and in spite of her fears to the contrary had seemed to accept the situation, so really it had only been a matter of time before the patients followed suit. But were they that transparent, she and Tom? Were their feelings reflected right there on their faces for all to see? And if so, did it matter, provided it didn't interfere with their work?

With a little sigh she took a sip of her coffee, reflecting as she did so on the past few weeks.

She had taken Natalie's advice, allowing her relationship with Tom to unfold naturally, and she had enjoyed every precious moment of it, keeping her fears for the future firmly under control and just allowing herself to be happy for the first time in two years. There had been many family occasions—meals together either at Copse End or Kingfishers and they had all gone to watch Joe play rugby for his school and had cheered themselves hoarse when his team had won. They had gone to the coast again, all of them this time, and Tom had made a barbeque on the beach. Later they had sat in the moonlight in the shadow of the rocks while Tom had strummed a guitar. They had all gone to see Siobhan in her school play, even Aunt Bessie, and Kate knew how pleased Siobhan had been when afterwards she'd hugged her daughter and Siobhan had said, 'That was great, you all coming—just like we were a real family.' All of those moments were precious, the kind of moments that made memories that could be taken out and enjoyed again and again right down the years. But for Kate even more precious than those shared family moments were the times that she and Tom spent alone.

He took her out again, several times, to restaurants and

once to a hotel in the Cotswolds where they stayed over-
night, but the only place that they could truly relax and be
completely alone was at Kingfishers when Joe and
Francesca were with their mother and Siobhan and Connor
with Aunt Bessie. On these occasions Kate didn't stay the
night, feeling this would be unfair on Aunt Bessie, and in
some strange way this seemed to make the few hours they
spent together even more precious.

'I don't want you to go,' he said more than once when,
after making love, he would reach out for her again.

They had talked of their relationship and where it was
going, of course they had, just as they had talked about
commitment and the future. 'We'll take it slowly,' Tom
had said at the beginning, mindful, no doubt, of her be-
reavement and whether or not she was fully over Liam's
death and also, Kate was certain, mindful of his own fears
about being able to trust anyone again. But as time had
gone on they had inevitably found themselves talking of
the future and of being together.

He had told her he loved her, once, deep in the night
when he had called her name as they had shared wonderful
sex together.

'But there are so many problems,' she had said on another occasion as they had lain in bed together after a particularly mind-shattering hour of making love. 'There are
your children, and there are mine, there is your house and
there is Aunt Bessie and Copse End. I couldn't just leave
her, Tom, especially after her being so good to us.'

'No, of course not,' he'd agreed. 'We need to think
things through thoroughly before we do anything, but in
the meantime…'

Kate smiled now as she recalled how he had reached out
for her again, pulling her on top of him and laughing up

into her eyes. Surely there was nothing now that could destroy such happiness?

'Kate?' She looked up sharply to find Tom in the open doorway of her office, and because of the erotic nature of the thoughts she'd been having she felt the colour flush her cheeks. Tom saw it, too, and he came right into the office, shutting the door firmly behind him. 'What is it?' he said softly.

'Nothing,' she protested.

'Yes, there was,' he persisted. 'I know that look. Come on, tell me, I want to know.'

'I was thinking about us, if you must know, Tom Fielding,' she said with a defiant tilt of her chin, looking up into his face.

'Ah,' he said, 'that's all right, then. Like I say, I know that look that was on your face and I would hate to think that you were thinking about any other man while you were looking that way.'

'Tom, there is no other man,' she said softly. 'You know that, I know that, everyone knows that—for heaven's sake, even the patients know.'

'The patients?' He looked faintly alarmed. 'Was that what that was all about back there?' He jerked his thumb over his shoulder and when Kate nodded ruefully, he threw back his head and laughed. 'Well,' he said at last, 'what does it matter? I don't care who knows. As far as I'm concerned, I'm the happiest man alive.'

'I'm glad to hear it, Mr Fielding,' Kate stood up and smoothed down her uniform, 'but, believe it or not, we have work to do.'

'Oh?' said Tom. 'Do we have to? I was about to suggest we sneak off to Kingfishers for an hour or two.'

'Mr Fielding! Whatever next? With Mrs Jackson about

to give birth and Ros Burton's twins imminent, I don't know how you can think of such a thing!'

'Quite easily actually,' said Tom with a grin, 'but it looks like I shall have to restrain myself, at least for the time being. But I warn you, Kate Ryan, it won't last for long—either you come over to my place after work or I shall have to come and get you.'

Because Kate was so happy the blow, when it came, had far more impact than it once might have done. As with so many of these things, it came with no warning. The day seemed no different from any other. It had started with a busy shift on Maternity with two births and a Caesarean section, and the only thing which seemed to make the day any more significant than any other came in the news that Maggie Sumner's baby had successfully come through surgery to repair a hole in his heart. Maggie herself had also recently undergone cardiac surgery for a rare condition, which she had apparently been born with but which hadn't manifested until she had gone into labour. Tom's relief that he hadn't been in any way to blame for Maggie's collapse was enormous, and his reaction was similar when they received the good news about baby Stuart.

'Thank God they are both all right,' he said to Kate as they shared a lunchtime sandwich in the staff canteen.

'I don't think the public have any idea what we go through sometimes,' said Kate.

The shift ended without further incident and Kate went home to Copse End. She and Tom hadn't made any plans for that evening but they were both looking forward to one of their family weekends. Aunt Bessie was in the garden, deadheading her rose bushes, and she greeted Kate cheerily.

'I'll just get changed,' said Kate, 'then I'll make some tea. Are the children in?'

'Siobhan is,' Aunt Bessie replied, 'but Connor had swimming after school.'

She found Siobhan lying full length on her bed, talking into her mobile phone. Kate smiled at her daughter then hurried to her own bedroom to change. She was just brushing her hair when she caught sight of her daughter's reflection in the mirror. Siobhan was standing in the open doorway.

'That was Francesca,' she said.

'Oh?' said Kate. 'Is she all right?'

'Yes, I think so…although, no, actually I don't think she was.'

'Why?' The hairbrush poised in her hand, Kate turned to face Siobhan.

'There's been a huge fight apparently between her mother and Max.'

'Well, I shouldn't worry too much,' said Kate. 'Francesca has told you before that they are always fighting.'

'This sounds a bit worse than usual,' said Siobhan, holding out her hand and splaying her fingers in order to study the glittery nail polish she had just applied. 'Francesca said there was a lot of swearing and shouting and slamming about, then Max packed a couple of holdalls and roared off in his Jag.'

'I expect he'll be back,' said Kate.

'We'll see,' said Siobhan.

As her daughter ambled back to her bedroom and Kate turned to the mirror again, she felt the first twinge of unease.

This feeling persisted throughout the evening until at last she received a call from Tom.

'Kate?' he said, and her heart gave the little flutter that it always did at the sound of his voice.

'Tom, hello.'

'Kate, I have a bit of a problem.'

'Is it the children?' she asked quickly.

'In a way.' He paused. 'Have you heard anything?'

'Yes,' she said. 'Francesca phoned Siobhan.'

'What did she tell her?' he asked.

'That her mother and Max had had a huge fight and Max had stormed out. I told her he would probably soon be back.'

'I think there's a bit more to it this time,' he said, and Kate felt the second pang of unease. 'Jennifer has got herself into a terrible state and Joe and Francesca are both pretty upset. I'm going over there to see if I can help sort things out. I thought I'd let you know in case you were trying to contact me.'

'Yes, all right, Tom,' she replied flatly.

'I'll see you tomorrow,' he said.

'Yes…'

'Oh, and, Kate?'

'Yes?'

'I love you,' he said.

'I love you, too,' she said, but in spite of that her heart was heavy with foreboding as she replaced the receiver.

Kate spent a troubled night, tossing and turning and lying awake for hours as all sorts of mental pictures filled her mind and endless questions teemed through her brain. What had Tom found when he had arrived at Jennifer's home? Just how distraught had his ex-wife been? And how upset were Joe and Francesca? What would happen next? Would Max go back? Come to that, where had he gone? On and on the questions went as Kate fitfully drifted in and out of sleep.

She must have slept more soundly towards dawn because when she awoke she found she had overslept and felt tired and heavy-eyed. Her telephone remained ominously silent and when, unable to contain herself any longer, she tried Tom's number there was no reply.

Maybe, she comforted herself, he had already left for work, but when she arrived at the hospital it was to be told that Mr Fielding had rescheduled his appointments for that day and had taken a few days' annual leave.

'Kate, are you all right?' asked Natalie halfway through the morning. 'You look really tired.'

'I am,' Kate admitted. 'I didn't sleep too well last night.'

'Any reason for that?' Natalie raised her eyebrows. 'Nothing to do with a certain consultant cancelling his list this morning, by any chance?'

'Well, partly, I suppose, but I'm sorry, Natalie, it isn't something I can discuss, even with you.'

'OK,' Natalie replied, 'but you know where I am if you change your mind. All I will say is that you've been happier in the last few weeks than I've seen you in a very long time. I would hate for anything to spoil that.'

So would I, thought Kate as she made her way to the labour suite to assist with an imminent birth. And, really, she didn't know why she was worrying because, no doubt, by now everything would have sorted itself out. With that comforting thought uppermost in her mind, she turned her attention once more to the job in hand.

The patient, Nola Ayles, was a woman in her thirties and her baby was her third. Between contractions she managed to give Kate a potted version of her life history. It appeared her husband had left her after the birth of her second child and this third baby was the result of a relationship with a twenty-year-old man.

'Doesn't he want to be here for the birth?' asked Kate as she and Mary prepared for the baby's arrival.

'No.' Nola shook her head. 'I've finished with him,' she stated.

'Really?' Mary turned from the cot in surprise.

'Yes, it was a mistake—it would never have worked out. I thought I loved him but it wasn't real. Oh, it was exciting, there's no doubt about that, but it wouldn't have come to anything. I can see that now.'

'Does this mean you are on your own now?' asked Kate.

'Oh no. Kevin's come home—he's my husband,' Nola explained, so there could be no doubt. 'When he said he wanted to come back I gave Justin his marching orders. The kids are over the moon—they couldn't wait to have their dad back. And this little one…' She looked down at the huge mound of her abdomen. 'Well, Kev has said he'll bring it up as if it were his own.'

At her words Kate felt a sudden tug at her emotions as she thought of Tom and his children—would he go back to Jennifer for their sakes? But she mustn't think about that now, she told herself, firmly trying to dismiss the thought. She had a job to do and, besides, it was highly unlikely that would happen. But hearing Nola talk of her tangled relationships had thrown it all sharply into focus.

'Oh!' Nola suddenly gasped as she was seized by a fresh contraction. 'Here comes another one. I'm going to push this time, Sister…'

Nola's baby was safely delivered an hour later, a healthy boy who cried loud and lustily until he and his mother were transferred from the labour suite to the postnatal ward. But for Kate, even though Nola had gone, the disturbing thoughts she had stirred up refused to go away, and by the time she came off duty she was desperate for news of Tom.

He phoned her almost as soon as she arrived home. It was such a relief to hear his voice that for a moment words seemed to stick in her throat.

'Kate?' he said, when he must have misunderstood her silence. 'Are you all right?'

'Yes, Tom,' she managed to say at last. 'How are things with you?'

'A bit traumatic,' he admitted. 'Jennifer was in a terrible state when I got there so I called her GP. He gave her something to calm her down but I felt I had to stay there—for Joe and Francesca's sakes as much as for Jennifer, really.'

Kate's hand tightened on the receiver. 'Yes, of course,' she heard herself say. 'So what's happening now?'

'The children went to school and I've come home. I'll be picking them up in a while—after that, I'm not sure.'

'Do you know what happened?' she asked. 'About the fight, I mean, and Max leaving?'

'The usual thing, apparently,' Tom replied. 'It was about his wife not giving him a divorce so that he and Jennifer can marry.'

'But surely that isn't his fault—is it?' she asked uncertainly.

'You try telling Jennifer that—she simply won't listen to reason. I think deep down she believes that Max will eventually go back to his wife—that is, if he hasn't done so already.'

'Do you think that's a possibility?' she asked. The sense of foreboding that had been with her ever since Siobhan had told her about Max leaving home seemed to be gaining momentum by the hour.

'Could be,' Tom replied. 'We don't really know where he is. Jennifer thought he might be at his chambers but when we enquired they said he hadn't been in all day.'

'It's all a bit of a mess, isn't it?' she said helplessly.

'Yes, it is,' Tom admitted. 'But it's not your problem, Kate, and I don't want you to worry about it. I'll try and sort things out over the next few days so, please, bear with me for the time being.'

'Of course I will, Tom,' she said. 'And, please, let me know if there is anything I can do.'

'Thanks, Kate,' he said, and his voice softened. 'I'll let you know. I have to go now and get over to Waterhouse to pick up Joe and Francesca.'

Once again, before he hung up he told her he loved her, but still Kate felt unsettled, as if all the happiness of the past few weeks was about to come crashing down around her ears.

In the end she confided in Aunt Bessie later that evening after both Siobhan and Connor were in bed and she had gone downstairs to share a bedtime drink with her aunt. She hadn't intended saying anything but Aunt Bessie had asked her point blank what was wrong.

'I know something is wrong, Kate,' she said firmly when Kate tried to deny it. 'You seem to forget I've known you since you were a baby. I watched you grow up. I knew then when something was wrong in your world, and I know now.'

'It's Tom,' said Kate, at last as she peered miserably into her mug and watched the froth settle on her Horlicks.

'I thought it might be,' Aunt Bessie replied calmly, 'so come on, tell me, what's the problem?'

'His ex-wife's boyfriend has left her and may have gone back to his wife.'

'So why should that pose a problem for Tom?'

'Apparently she is in a terrible state and Tom went there last night. He called her GP who gave her a sedative, and Tom thought he should stay there with Joe and Francesca.'

'Very wise,' said Aunt Bessie philosophically, 'especially if their mother was in such a state as all that.' She paused and looked at Kate over the top of her glasses. 'But I'm still not sure what the problem is.'

'Neither am I really.' Kate shook her head. 'Tom said he was picking Joe and Francesca up from school. Maybe he will be taking them back to his place... I don't really know.'

'And their mother...?'

'Maybe,' said Kate again. 'He didn't say.'

'And that's what you're worrying about? That somehow this situation might bring them back together?'

'I don't know... I suppose... Oh, I really don't know.' Helplessly Kate stared at her aunt. 'I just have this awful feeling—it's been there ever since Siobhan told me that Max had walked out on Jennifer—that somehow this could be the start of Tom and his ex-wife getting back together.'

'Kate, this is only supposition on your part,' said Aunt Bessie firmly. 'You don't know for sure that this is what will happen, now, do you?'

'No,' Kate admitted, 'I don't.'

'And has Tom ever given you any reason to suppose that he might take his ex-wife back?'

'Not really,' said Kate slowly, 'although I have wondered whether he would give his marriage another try for the sake of the children. She did come back to him once but it didn't last and she left again.'

'There has to be a limit to that sort of toing and froing,' said Aunt Bessie firmly. 'And I still think you are worrying unnecessarily.'

'I hope you're right.'

'Kate, I want to ask you something,' said Aunt Bessie after a moment. 'You can tell me to mind my own business if you like but I'm going to ask anyway.'

'Go on,' said Kate with a weak smile.

'Do you love Tom?' asked Aunt Bessie.

'Yes, I think I do,' Kate replied. 'I really didn't think it would happen—not after Liam—and it didn't exactly happen with a crash of cymbals this time. Instead, it sort of crept up on me slowly, if you know what I mean.'

'Yes, I do know what you mean,' said Aunt Bessie. 'It was like that between your uncle and me.'

'Really?' said Kate in surprise. 'I thought you two had been childhood sweethearts.'

'Oh, we had,' said Aunt Bessie quickly. 'Then I met someone else and, believe me, it was the crashing cymbals variety, but it ended almost as quickly as it had begun. Your uncle was there to pick up the pieces and very gradually I came to realise he was the one for me.' A far-off, dreamy look had come into her eyes as she'd been speaking, then, as if she'd suddenly became aware of the silence between them, she seemed to give herself a little shake. 'So you love this man,' she said. 'And what about him? Does he love you?'

'He's told me he does—' Kate began, but Aunt Bessie cut her short.

'Well, what more do you want, for heaven's sake?' she said. 'You have to trust him, Kate. If he truly loves you he will sort things out. Now, finish your drink, get yourself to bed and have a good night's sleep. I'm sure things will look much better in the morning.'

And they might have done, but just as Kate was dropping off to sleep she felt a light touch on her hand and, opening her eyes, found Siobhan beside her bed.

'Siobhan? What is it?' She was instantly wide awake.

'Mum.' Siobhan looked troubled. 'I've just had a call from Francesca.'

'What?' Kate sat upright. 'At this time of night! Siobhan...' She peered at her bedside clock, its face just visible in the light from the landing. 'It's nearly midnight!'

'I know,' said Siobhan casually, as if that was the sort of thing they did all the time. They probably did, thought Kate, mentally making a note that some ground rules would have to be laid down over the use of mobile phones.

'What did she want?' she demanded.

'She wanted to tell me,' said Siobhan, 'that her mum and dad are getting back together again.'

CHAPTER TEN

KATE stared at her daughter, unable to speak as her worst fears threatened to become reality.

'She sounded really excited,' said Siobhan, 'but...' she paused. 'That isn't good for us, is it, Mum?' she added anxiously.

'Let's wait until we know for sure what's happening,' said Kate, struggling to stay calm.

'Francesca sounded sure,' said Siobhan. 'She said she heard her mum tell her dad that she wanted them to get back together again, that they owed it to them, Francesca and Joe, to give their marriage another go.'

'Siobhan, I'm not sure you should be repeating all this—' Kate began.

'But it's what she *said*,' said Siobhan. 'Francesca *heard* them. She said they were upset but that that was what was going to happen and that they would all be living together again.' She paused. 'Does it mean we won't be able to see them any more?' she demanded.

'I don't know,' said Kate, fighting to contain the sudden wave of nausea that swept over her as she grappled with the fact that in light of what her daughter had just revealed, her relationship with Tom might be finished. 'I expect you and Francesca would be able to still see each other—I don't really know,' she added helplessly. Suddenly she felt hopelessly inadequate at giving her daughter the reassurance she craved.

'But we wouldn't all be able to go out together again,

would we?' An anxious frown creased Siobhan's smooth forehead. 'Not as a family?'

'No, Siobhan, we wouldn't.' Kate took a deep breath in a supreme effort to control her emotions. 'If Tom and Francesca's mother get back together there is no way that *I* could see him again.'

'Oh, Mum!' wailed Siobhan, as the full implication of what was happening finally seemed to sink in. 'It isn't fair—just when things were good again.'

'I know,' said Kate, pushing her hair back from her face and looping it behind one ear. 'I know, but if that's what's going to happen, that's the way it will have to be.'

'But I think it's really mean of Francesca's mum,' said Siobhan. 'After all, she had that Max chap. Why couldn't they just stay together?'

'Things aren't always that simple,' said Kate. Suddenly she felt incredibly weary but she knew she had to talk to Siobhan for as long as her daughter needed to. 'Max's wife won't give him a divorce,' she explained at last, deciding there and then that Siobhan should be told the truth behind what was happening. 'That means he isn't free to marry Francesca's mother, and it's that that has been causing all the rows.'

'I still don't think it's fair.' Siobhan pouted. 'And what about Joe?' she demanded suddenly.

'What *about* Joe?'

'Well, you say I might still be able to see Francesca, but if I do it will probably be if we go riding.'

'Yes?'

'Joe doesn't go riding very much. I probably won't get to see him at all—ever!' she added dramatically.

'Siobhan, you don't know any of this for certain,' said Kate. 'Let's wait until tomorrow and see what we can find out then. Try and get to sleep now.'

Siobhan went back to her own room and possibly she slept, but for Kate the hours of uncertainty stretched endlessly ahead of her as, unable to take the advice she had given to her daughter, she agonised over what was happening. Her worst fears had finally materialised in that one brief statement uttered by her daughter—that Francesca had said that her mum and dad were getting back together again.

But was there any chance that Francesca could have got it wrong? It seemed unlikely if she had actually overheard her parents discussing it, so did that mean that even now Jennifer was back with Tom at Kingfishers? Was she sharing his bed, the very bed where she, Kate, had shared such wonderful lovemaking with Tom? And was it possible that Tom had been waiting for this moment all along, that to him she, Kate, had only been second best, good enough to spend time with but only until his wife returned to him?

And if that was the case, what of her? How would he end his relationship with her? In a phone call, brief and terse, or a letter, brutal and to the point? Or would it be face to face? Kate shuddered, not knowing how she would cope with such a moment, and when at last, after sleeping for a couple of hours, she awoke, it was to relive the misery all over again.

Thankfully she was on a late shift that day so when the phone rang she was still in her dressing-gown.

'Kate, it's me, Tom,' he said, and she clutched the receiver more tightly, convinced he was about to utter the words she had been dreading.

'Tom...?' She swallowed.

'You're on a late, aren't you?' he said.

'Yes.'

'I've decided to go in this morning,' he said. 'I can't

waste any more precious leave, but I wanted to speak to you first.'

Here it comes, she thought, bracing herself for the words that would destroy her world.

'I wanted to tell you I love you,' he said, and as Kate's heart turned over she almost dropped the receiver.

'Oh, Tom,' she whispered. 'I thought…'

'And I wanted to say that I've booked us into our special place in the Cotswolds next weekend. I really wanted it to be a surprise but I know you need to make plans. Anyway, I must go now. See you later, darling, and don't forget—I love you.'

He hung up, leaving Kate staring at the phone, her senses reeling. He still loved her after all. Francesca must have been mistaken. There was no way that Tom and Jennifer could be getting back together again, not when he was planning to take her to their favourite hotel in the Cotswolds.

Slowly she walked out of the sitting room and into Siobhan's bedroom, where she found her daughter packing her homework books into her school bag. It struck Kate that Siobhan still looked upset.

'Siobhan,' she said, going right into the room and shutting the door behind her, 'I think you may have either misunderstood what Francesca told you last night or maybe Francesca herself has somehow got things wrong. I've just spoken to Tom and he made no mention about him and Francesca's mother getting back together again.'

'Well, they are,' said Siobhan flatly. 'I know that for a fact because I rang Francesca early this morning and asked her. She said that she had asked her mother again and her mother said they were definitely getting back together again. Goodness knows why Tom hasn't told you.' She paused and looked at Kate. 'Unless he thinks he'll carry on seeing you as well.'

'Siobhan, that's a dreadful thing to say.' Kate stared at her daughter.

'Well, people do things like that, don't they?' said Siobhan with a shrug. 'Chloe said her dad has a girlfriend and her mum doesn't know anything about it. Anyway, I've got to go now or I'll miss the bus.' She dashed out of the room then came swiftly back again and gave Kate a kiss on the cheek. 'Don't worry, Mum,' she said. 'We managed without the Fieldings before. We'll manage without them again.'

After Siobhan had gone Kate sank down onto her daughter's bed with a sense of disbelief. Was that really what Tom was planning: to get back with Jennifer but to carry on seeing her as well? Surely he wouldn't do such a thing? On the other hand, if he and Jennifer were getting back together, and it now seemed certain that this was what was going to happen, why hadn't he told her just now when he had phoned? And why had he booked a weekend at their special hotel? The more she thought about it the more likely it seemed that what Siobhan had suggested was exactly what Tom had in mind.

Somehow Kate got through the rest of the morning but by the time she drove herself to work her indignation had reached boiling point. How dared Tom Fielding think he could use her like that? Just who did he think he was? He might well be the kingpin when it came to obstetrics and maternity but that didn't give him the right to ride roughshod over people's feelings and emotions. Why, he'd even had the gall to tell her he still loved her!

As she stalked onto the unit, spoiling for a fight, she was aware of Natalie's startled glance but she chose to ignore it, not wanting to be forced to give her friend any explanations until after she'd confronted Tom, knowing that if she did so her pent-up emotions might just get the better of her and her anger give way to despair.

It was just after she had assisted at a birth, supervising Melissa, and was on her way back to the nurses' station that she heard his voice. Her heart leapt as it always did, then, just as she was reminding herself not to be ridiculous, that this was the man who was two-timing her and that in future her heart would have to be more disciplined, he appeared from the postnatal ward. Dr Omar Nahum accompanied him and both men were deep in conversation, apparently discussing a case history. When he caught sight of Kate, Tom stopped, his gaze immediately seeking hers.

'Sister Ryan,' he said, and that same glint of amusement was there in his eyes, as it always was whenever they chanced to meet in the department, for all the world as if nothing had happened.

Kate felt the colour flood her face. How dared he act in this way when she had suffered such anguish? Did he not have any idea how she was feeling? Was he so wrapped up in his own affairs and the fact that his problems had resolved themselves that he remained oblivious to the hurt he caused others?

'Was there something you wanted, Mr Fielding?' she asked coldly, and was slightly gratified to see his look of surprise at her tone.

'Kate...?' he said, and frowned as if unable to understand her mood.

But what did he expect, for heaven's sake? she asked herself angrily. Surely he hadn't expected everything to carry on in exactly the same way?

'I was wondering,' he said, and he spoke softly now so that only she would hear. Even Omar, who was standing only a few feet away, wouldn't have any idea that it wasn't obstetric matters he spoke about. 'What did you think about my idea for the Cotswolds?'

She stared at him. 'I don't think, Mr Fielding,' she replied at last through gritted teeth, 'that you would want to know what I think.'

'Mr Fielding.' Omar stepped forward. 'We are due in a meeting.'

'Yes, Omar, I know,' Tom replied tersely. He turned back to Kate. 'What is it?' he asked in apparent bewilderment. 'Kate, what's wrong?'

'You know as well as I do,' she muttered back, 'and if you think we can just carry on the way we have been then you are very much mistaken.'

'Kate, I don't know what you mean,' he protested.

'Yes, you do,' she retorted, tears dangerously close now. 'You know only too well, just as you must now know that our relationship has to be over.'

'Kate!' He looked astounded. 'But why? I don't understand!'

'Tom, I can't believe you could think things could still be the same...' she choked.

'Mr Fielding...?' Dr Nahum was plainly becoming agitated.

'All right, Omar, I'm coming!' Tom began to back away from her. 'I have to go now, Kate,' he said, 'but I'll see you later. We'll talk then.'

Turning on her heel, Kate marched to her office where she closed the door firmly behind her. Only then did she allow herself to crumple as she sank down into the chair behind her desk and covered her face with her hands.

It looked as if she'd been right. He really had intended carrying on with their relationship, even though he and Jennifer were getting back together. So, if that was the case, when had he been planning to tell her that he and Jennifer were attempting to rebuild their marriage? When they were out with the children, over an intimate meal for two, or maybe at their favourite hotel when they were making love? Her heart twisted at the very thought. Could Tom really be that cruel?

She stared at the papers on her desk. Somehow she had to pull herself together and get on with her work. She felt terrible and would have liked nothing better than to go home, go to bed and pull the covers up over her head, but she couldn't do that. She had patients waiting, patients who were depending on her.

She took a deep breath and was about to get to her feet again when there came the sound of a light knock and Natalie put her head around the door.

'Kate?' she said. 'What is it? What's wrong?'

Kate took one look at her friend's sympathetic face and her resolve crumbled. She felt the tears well up in her eyes.

Without a word Natalie closed the door behind her and, coming right into the room, poured two mugs of coffee, handing one to Kate then sitting down in the chair opposite. 'Right,' she said, 'come on, what's this all about? And you needn't say nothing, because I know there's something. You haven't been yourself for the last couple of days, and this afternoon you look like death warmed up.'

'Thanks, Nat,' said Kate ruefully with a sniff. Leaning forward, she took a tissue from the box that Natalie pushed across the desk towards her. 'I really should be getting on...'

'You're not leaving this room until you tell me what is wrong,' said Natalie firmly. 'Any baby waiting to be born will just have to wait a bit longer.'

'It's Tom,' said Kate, after blowing her nose.

'Now tell me something I didn't know,' said Natalie dryly.

'You knew?' Kate looked at her in surprise.

'Well, let's just say I had a pretty good idea. You've been like a dog with two tails ever since you two got together then suddenly all is gloom and doom. So come on, tell me, what's he done?'

'It's not exactly anything he's done,' Kate began uncertainly. 'It's his ex-wife...'

'What's she got to do with anything?' Natalie frowned. 'Surely she's history.'

'That's what I thought,' replied Kate, 'but now it appears she wants to have another go at making their marriage work.'

'And Tom's going along with this?' Natalie sounded incredulous.

'Apparently so.' Kate shrugged. 'Oh, Nat, I've had this fear all along. I was always afraid that he still loved Jennifer and that if ever she wanted to go back to him he would jump at the chance.'

'But what about her bloke—the one she left Tom for in the first place?'

'Gone back to his wife apparently,' said Kate miserably.

'Oh, hell...' said Natalie. 'Oh, Kate, I'm sorry, I really am. I really thought that you and Tom...'

'I know,' said Kate. 'So did I.'

'Has he just told you it's all over? Was that what all that was about just now?'

'No.' Kate shook her head. 'I told *him* it's over. But would you believe he still seems to think we can carry on in the same way.'

'No!' Natalie stared at her.

'Yes, he was talking about us going away for a couple of days, just as if nothing had happened, as if it shouldn't make any difference to us just because he's back with his wife. I tell you, Natalie, I could have found myself in a situation like that one with Sara Millington and Philip Browne, where he was flitting between her and his wife.'

'Honestly! Men!' Natalie rolled her eyes. 'Well, I hope you told him,' she added vehemently. 'Some of them seem to think they can get away with murder.'

'Oh, I told him all right,' said Kate bitterly. 'There's no way I could go on seeing him under those circumstances.'

'Absolutely,' Natalie replied. Draining her mug, she stood up. 'I must get on,' she said, 'but listen, Kate, you take your time—don't go back out there until you're good and ready. And try not to let this get you down too much. There are plenty more fish in the sea.'

'Just give me a minute, that's all.' As the door shut behind Natalie Kate finished her coffee. Standing up, she smoothed down her uniform and, after a quick but far from reassuring glance in the mirror, she took a deep breath, squared her shoulders and prepared to set foot on the unit once more. There was no way that either her staff or her patients would know that, although she appeared her usual calm and controlled self on the outside, inside her heart was breaking as she grappled to come to terms with the fact that the relationship she and Tom had shared and which had come to mean so much to her had obviously meant nothing to him.

Somehow she managed to avoid Tom for the rest of her shift—usually that would have been impossible but on that particular day he came out of his meeting and had to go straight into Theatre to perform emergency surgery on a young woman suffering an ectopic pregnancy. She saw him in passing, of course, but she managed to avoid eye contact with him, at the same time knowing he was desperately trying to attract her attention. What he thought he was going to achieve she had no idea. Maybe he wanted to apologise, she thought grimly, but if that was the case she knew

she was in no mood to hear such an apology, let alone
accept one.

Already it was beginning to dawn on Kate how difficult
it was going to be to carry on working with Tom in the
future, the future that would mean him living with Jennifer
again and settling down once more as a family man. And
as she drove away from the hospital after her shift, down
the tree-lined avenue, in desperation she found herself wondering whether she should start looking for another job. It
was the last thing she wanted to do. She loved her work at
Ellie's and she knew that to secure another similar post in
a maternity department it would mean either moving house
or commuting miles each day, both prospects that filled her
with dread. On the other hand how could she bear to carry
on, seeing Tom every day, hearing his voice, maybe oc-
casionally having to touch him, all the while knowing that
at the end of each day he would return to his wife?

Really, she should be pleased for him, she told herself
firmly, and for Joe and Francesca—especially Francesca
who had so desperately wanted her parents to get back together again. And in the normal course of events she would
have been pleased. If it had been any other couple she had
heard about who had decided to give their marriage another
try after having divorced, she would have been delighted.
But this was Tom, the only man since Liam she had given
her heart to. This was different...

When she reached home it was to find that Aunt Bessie
was entertaining her friend Dorothy in her sitting room and
the children were upstairs, watching television.

'Would you like a cup of tea, dear?' asked Aunt Bessie
as Kate looked round the door to say hello.

'No,' Kate replied. 'If you don't mind, I need some air.
I'm going to take a walk in the copse.' The last thing she
wanted in her present state of mind was to have to sit and

listen to Aunt Bessie and her friend reminisce about the past.

It was deliciously cool in the copse, the evening sunlight filtering through the leaves of the sycamore trees and dappling the mossy pathway ahead. Apart from the occasional rustlings of some small animal as it foraged for food, the only sound to be heard was the song of a bird as it accompanied Kate, flying alongside her from branch to branch. The sheer peace of the woods helped to calm the turmoil of her thoughts, and by the time she reached the five-bar gate at the boundary she was able to lean on the top bar and, in a quieter mood, gaze out over the rich gold of the ripening crops in the field beyond. So lost did she become in her thoughts and reflections that she failed to hear any sound on the soft path behind her, and by the time she heard her name spoken he was almost beside her.

She turned sharply to find Tom there. 'Oh!' she gasped. 'You made me jump. No one comes to these woods...'

'I'm sorry,' he said. 'I should have called out or something.'

'How did you know I was here?' Suddenly she was angry that he should have come here to this private place, the place where she was striving to restore her peace of mind when it had been he who had been responsible for destroying that peace in the first place.

'I went to the house,' he said. 'I saw Aunt Bessie and she told me I would find you here.'

'She had no right to tell you that,' Kate began, still angry, irritated even by his reference to Aunt Bessie—as if he still had the right to call her that. 'I wanted to be on my own.'

'Kate, please.' He reached out his hand but she ignored it, turning back to her contemplation of the corn and the bright splashes of scarlet from the poppies that edged a pathway through the centre of the field. 'Please, tell me what I'm supposed to have done.'

'What you are supposed to have done?' Incredulously she half turned to him again. 'Well, if you don't know…!' she said in exasperation.

'Kate…' He spread his hands. 'I have no idea, really I don't. The last time we were together everything was wonderful between us and then this afternoon you tell me we are finished. Can you explain why?'

Kate stared at him. 'You really think,' she said slowly, carefully, considering each word, 'that you and I can carry on seeing each other?'

'I can't see why not.' He frowned.

'Well, let's just consider for a moment. If I was to agree to that,' said Kate, struggling to remain calm, 'which I hasten to add that I'm not, but let's suppose I did and we carried on seeing one another, no doubt secretly this time—'

'Why secretly?' He looked bewildered now.

'Presumably even you wouldn't want your wife finding out that you were having an affair behind her back,' she retorted.

'My wife?' he protested. 'I don't have a wife.'

'No, but—'

'Kate!' He interrupted her, then took a deep breath. 'Can we start from the beginning, please? Somewhere along the line you have lost me.'

'OK.' She shrugged.

'So tell me first, please, why did you tell me it was all over between us?'

'Because of Jennifer,' she replied.

'Jennifer? What's she got to do with anything?'

'Tom, please.' Kate held up her hands, the gesture one of helpless despair. 'This is getting ridiculous. There is simply no way that I can continue having a relationship with you now that you and Jennifer are getting back together again.'

He stared at her. 'Me and Jennifer getting—?'

'Yes, Tom,' Kate interrupted him, 'and before you say any more I'd just like to say that I understand why you are doing it. I know what it will mean to your children, especially Francesca, and I wouldn't want to be the one to prevent that from happening. But you have to understand that there can be no more between us. In fact, I'm amazed and annoyed to think that you should even think such a thing could be possible—'

'Whoa! Hold on!' Reaching out, he took her wrists, imprisoning them. 'Stop, Kate, please. Right there. Now,' he said when she stopped her tirade and he had her attention again, 'where on earth did you get the idea that Jennifer and I were getting back together again?'

'Siobhan told me,' she said.

'And who told Siobhan?' he asked, raising his eyebrows.

'Francesca.'

'Ah,' he said. 'And did she happen to say where Francesca had got this idea from?'

'Yes.' Kate frowned. 'Siobhan told me that Francesca had overheard a conversation between you and Jennifer and that she'd heard her mother say that she thought that now was the right time for you all to get back together again or something like that. But, whatever it was, she *heard* it, Tom.'

'She may well have heard her mother's side of that particular conversation,' said Tom, 'but she certainly didn't hear mine.'

'What do you mean?' Kate stared at him, almost oblivious now to the fact that he still had hold of her wrists, so intent was she on hearing what he was saying.

'It was on the phone,' Tom replied, 'and Francesca was with her mother.'

'But did Jennifer say those things—that she still loved you and that you should try again?'

'Yes,' he admitted, 'she did. But it was at a time when she was extremely upset. Max had just walked out on her— I told you all about that.'

'Yes.' Kate nodded. 'Yes, you did.'

'And I also told you that this has happened before?'

She nodded again.

'Jennifer always seeks me out when things are going wrong,' said Tom. 'I'm a sort of safety net for her, if you like—or rather, I have been in the past. This time things were different.'

'Why?' Her voice was barely more than a whisper as she stared at him.

'Because this time I had you,' he said simply. 'When she started making her usual demands and suggestions about us trying again for the sake of the children, and that deep down it was really me she had loved all along, I cut her short and told her that this time things had changed, that I'd met you and fallen in love with you. I also told her that the love I had once felt for her had died a long time ago and it would be pointless to try and resurrect it.'

'What did she say?' asked Kate faintly.

'She hung up on me,' he replied. 'But she'll get over it, Kate. I know she will. Just as I know that in no time at all she and Max will be back together again.'

'You think so?' she asked dubiously.

'I'd stake my life on it,' he said. 'So you needn't go feeling guilty in any way, thinking that you are preventing my children from seeing their parents get back together again. It isn't going to happen, Kate. It never was, not in the past because of Jennifer's feelings for Max, and not now because of my feelings for you.'

Kate stared at Tom, almost unable to believe what he was saying, and then slowly it began to dawn on her how she had misjudged him. 'Oh, Tom,' she said helplessly, 'I'm so sorry. I should have trusted you. It's just that the thing I had dreaded seemed to be happening right under my nose.'

'What had you been dreading?' he asked, his expression mystified.

'That it was Jennifer you loved all along and that really you were just waiting for her to come back to you.'

'Kate—it was never like that,' he said softly. 'I stopped loving Jennifer a long time ago.'

'Oh, Tom,' she whispered, 'can you ever forgive me?'

'There's nothing to forgive,' he said lightly. 'I would probably have felt exactly the same if it had been the other way round.'

'It was just that Siobhan said Francesca seemed so sure... And, Tom, she was so excited. Why, even this morning she spoke to Siobhan and said that her mother had told her that you were all going to live together again. Why would she tell Francesca something like that?'

'I don't know. Maybe she thought by telling Francesca it would get back to you and destroy the love we have. Jennifer does have a very jealous streak and she wouldn't be able to cope with our happiness, especially now when she is on her own. Or perhaps she thought she could talk me round,' he added grimly. 'But even if she could and we got back together, it would only be until she decided it was all a big mistake. I can see I need to have another word with Jennifer,' he went on. 'She must understand she is not to say such things to the children when there is no likelihood of them happening.'

'Poor Francesca,' said Kate. 'How must she be feeling now?'

'Leave Francesca to me,' said Tom. 'I'll talk to her and I think you will find she will come round in no time at all. She loves the time we all spend together and I think she would have been pretty upset if all that had come to an end.'

'That's what Siobhan was worried about,' said Kate, 'and about the fact that she might no longer see Joe.'

'Kate.' Still holding her hands, he looked down into her eyes. 'I think we need to be more certain about the future when we talk to the children. Let's face it, they do tend to like to have everything cut and dried, don't they?'

'Well, they certainly like to feel secure,' Kate agreed. 'I dare say Francesca was feeling insecure because of her mother's volatile relationship and because she knows you are alone. I know she hates that because she told Siobhan once…'

'Maybe now is the time, then, to tell her that I won't be alone any longer and that soon she will be part of another, bigger family. What do you think?'

Kate was aware that her heart had started to thump rather loudly. 'I think,' she said, hoping Tom couldn't hear it, 'that might certainly help…'

'In that case, my darling Kate, will you marry me?' Taking her face between his hands, he gazed into her eyes. 'You don't need to give me an answer now. This must have come as a bit of a shock to you and it wasn't at all how I'd planned it—it was meant to be champagne and our special hotel. But, please, at least will you promise me that you will think about it?'

'I don't need time to think about it,' she said softly, reaching up and gently kissing the corner of his mouth. 'I love you, Tom, and knowing you feel the same way about me is enough.'

'You mean…?' His face flushed with pleasure for a moment, making him appear vulnerable, boyish even, and Kate's heart went out to him. To think that this man, her boss and Ellie's rather serious-minded consultant obstetrician, should have such a tender, caring side to him. But, then, hadn't she always suspected that there was rather more to Tom Fielding than met the eye? With a little sigh of utter happiness she parted her lips for his kiss.

'Well, I thought it all went rather well, didn't you?' Tom smiled at Kate across the sun lounge at Kingfishers while from outside the shouts and laughter of the children indicated they were enjoying themselves in the swimming pool. During the last two days he and Kate had set about telling people of their future plans. They had told their children when they'd all been together, then each of them had spent time alone with their own children, then with each other's children. They had been very careful not to underestimate Joe and Francesca's feelings for their mother or Siobhan and Connor's for Liam.

Predictably it had been Francesca who had been the most wary. 'Where will we live?' had been her first question.

'You will continue to live with your mother,' Tom had replied patiently, 'but you can come to us at Kingfishers as often as you like.'

'It'll be great!' Siobhan had said, her eyes shining.

'Will I be able to swim in the pool?' Connor had asked.

'Every day if you like,' Tom had replied.

'If we're going to live with Tom, what about Aunt Bessie?'

Suddenly the reality of the situation seemed to hit Siobhan and she voiced the fear that had been uppermost in Kate's mind ever since Tom had asked her to marry him. Aunt Bessie had been so good to her and to the children since Liam's death and the last thing in the world she wanted to do was to leave her alone now at Copse End just when she had got used to them all living there. They had even considered Tom moving in there, but that would have posed a problem when Joe and Francesca came to stay because there wasn't really enough room.

In the end the problem solved itself. When Tom and Kate went together to tell Aunt Bessie, she proceeded to tell them that she would be offering the upstairs apartment to her friend Dorothy, who had to look for alternative accommodation. 'So, dears,' she said, her face beaming, 'you mustn't worry about me. I will be just fine. The children can still come to me after school, and Copse End will always be here for you, Kate, just as I said it would. All the two of you have to do is to be happy.'

Needless to say, Natalie echoed Aunt Bessie's sentiments when Kate broke the news to her, albeit in a rather more robust way.

'*Yes!*' she cried. 'I knew it. Oh, Kate, that's brilliant! I'm so, so happy for you!'

And now, as Kate looked at Tom and her heart suffused with love for him, she couldn't quite believe that it was happening, that she was being given yet another chance at happiness. But it was happening and the reality was right there as he reached out and took her hand.

'Happy?' he said.

'Oh, yes,' she replied with a little sigh, 'so very, very happy. Are you?' she added anxiously.

'Yes,' he said, 'although…'

'Although what?' She sat up a little straighter and stared at him, concerned now that there might be some other problem they hadn't considered.

'I would be even happier if you were to come back later this evening,' he said softly.

'Really, Mr Fielding,' she said with mock severity, 'are you suggesting what I think you might be suggesting?'

'I don't know, Sister Ryan,' he replied solemnly. 'I was merely thinking we could perhaps start planning the details of our wedding, that's all.'

'Oh, well, that's all right, then,' said Kate with a low chuckle. 'For one moment there I thought you might have been suggesting something altogether different.'

'Heavens,' he replied, squeezing her hand, 'I don't know whatever gave you that idea. So…' He paused and his gaze sought and held hers. 'What time do you think you could come back?'

'Shall we say nine o'clock?' she said softly.

'Nine o'clock it is,' he replied.

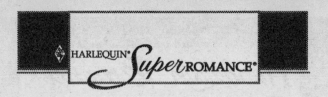

HARLEQUIN *Presents*

The world's bestselling romance series...
The series that brings you your favorite authors,
month after month:

Helen Bianchin...Emma Darcy
Lynne Graham...Penny Jordan
Miranda Lee...Sandra Marton
Anne Mather...Carole Mortimer
Susan Napier...Michelle Reid

and many more uniquely talented authors!

Wealthy, powerful, gorgeous men...
Women who have feelings just like your own...
The stories you love, set in exotic, glamorous locations...

HARLEQUIN *Presents*

Seduction and passion guaranteed!

HARLEQUIN®
INTRIGUE

WE'LL LEAVE YOU BREATHLESS!

If you've been looking for thrilling tales of
contemporary passion and sensuous love stories
with taut, edge-of-the-seat suspense—then
you'll love Harlequin Intrigue!

Every month, you'll meet four new heroes
who are guaranteed to make your spine tingle
and your pulse pound. With them you'll enter
into the exciting world of Harlequin Intrigue—
where your life is on the line
and so is your heart!

THAT'S INTRIGUE—
ROMANTIC SUSPENSE
AT ITS BEST!

HARLEQUIN®

Makes any time special ®